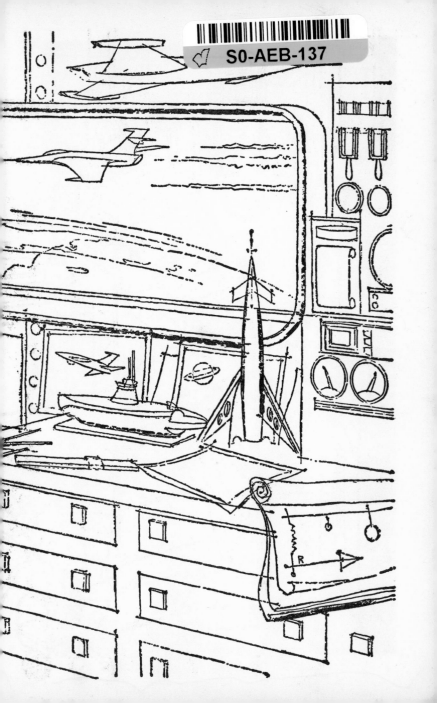

TOM SWIFT AND HIS POLAR-RAY DYNASPHERE

An unidentified rocket ship crashes into the Swifts' outpost in space and vanishes before Tom can track it down.

Shortly after comes the startling news that a Mars probe rocket, vital to the United States space program, has failed to respond to signals to bring it back to earth. Tom is confident that with his latest invention—the polar-ray dynasphere—he can retrieve the stranded missile. But a web of espionage threatens his plan. A clue to the solution of the mystery prompts Tom to accept an invitation from young Prince Jahan to visit his native land of Vishnapur in the snow-peaked Himalayas north of India.

In this remote Oriental kingdom, Tom and his pal Bud Barclay visit a strange lake of death and sight the tracks of a weird monster said to prowl the lake at night. Tom conceives an ingenious plan for draining the poison lake with the dynasphere mounted aboard his new spacecraft, the *Dyna Ranger,* so that the valley may be turned into valuable farmland.

Fireball missiles and a hairbreadth encounter with a charging tiger are only two of the perils that confront the daring young inventor in this colorful, thrill-packed adventure.

"It's the monster!" Bud gasped

THE NEW TOM SWIFT Jr. ADVENTURES

TOM SWIFT
AND HIS POLAR-RAY
DYNASPHERE

BY VICTOR APPLETON II

ILLUSTRATED BY EDWARD MORITZ

GROSSET & DUNLAP

NEW YORK PUBLISHERS

PRINTED IN THE UNITED STATES OF AMERICA

CONTENTS

CHAPTER   PAGE

1   SPACE CRASH   1
2   ACCIDENTAL BLACKOUT   10
3   THE BRONZE BUDDHA   18
4   A MARTIAN MYSTERY   28
5   A HAIR-RAISING EXPERIMENT   38
6   THE SAFFRON CLUE   48
7   THE GODDESS OF DOOM   55
8   A ROYAL WELCOME   65
9   THE POISON LAKE   73
10   SKY SHOW   84
11   FLIGHT INTO DANGER   93
12   TIGER HUNT   101
13   DEADLY QUILLS   110
14   THE KIDNAPPED SATELLITE   120
15   ROCKET CHASE   130
16   THE LAKE MONSTER   139
17   KALI'S SECRET   147
18   HIDDEN LAIR   155
19   ROCKET ROOST   163
20   PLANET PRIZE   172

CHAPTER I

SPACE CRASH

THE intercom in the astronomy wing of the Swifts' space outpost buzzed like an angry hornet. A lanky blond youth with crew-cut hair and steel-blue eyes turned away from an electronic console to answer the call. "Tom Swift here."

"An unidentified spacecraft is approaching!" came the excited voice of Ken Horton, commander of the outpost. "It's on a collision course!"

"Have you challenged it over the radio?"

"We've tried, but we get no response."

Husky, dark-haired Bud Barclay saw the startled look on his chum's face as Tom left the intercom. "What's wrong, pal?"

Tom relayed the frightening news. Then the young inventor quickly trained a small optical telescope in the direction Ken had indicated and brought the image into focus.

1

"Good night!" Tom muttered. "That thing must be out of control! Look, Bud!"

A weird, needle-nosed rocket ship, with a pale yellow hull and a high, vertical tail fin, was hurtling straight toward them.

Tom darted back to the intercom. "Sound a general alarm, Ken! Muster all hands in the hub!" Then he and Bud dashed through the long observatory toward the central compartment.

The outpost in space, orbiting 22,300 miles above the earth, was shaped like a gigantic twelve-spoked wheel. Tom had designed the station as a factory, where his solar-charged batteries could be exposed to the sun's unshielded rays.

Each spoke served a separate purpose. One was equipped for space medical research; another was the crew's living quarters; from a third, radio and TV broadcasts were relayed to earth.

Out of each spoke, the crew poured into the central hub. White-faced, they watched the mysterious rocket ship streaking closer and closer on the television monitor.

Ken Horton, a slender young man with dark, close-cropped hair, barked out a command. "Check all compartment doors. Make sure they're sealed! If that ship crashes into the station, an air loss could wipe us out!"

"Are you still trying to contact it?" Tom asked, glancing at the radioman who was seated just behind Horton in the central control booth.

Ken nodded grimly. "Pete's been calling over a broad band of frequencies. No answer!"

"The crew could have bailed out," Tom said. "Or passed out—from space sickness."

Another thought crossed Tom's mind. The strange craft might be robot-controlled! Perhaps deliberately launched by some enemy in a fiendish attack against the space outpost!

"Our meteorite repelatron may help," Tom said. This invention, which beamed out a repulsion ray, was designed to ward off swarms of micrometeorites. The beam was not powerful enough to repel a spaceship coming at such tremendous speed, but it might lessen the impact.

There was no time to don space suits. The hurtling craft loomed larger and larger on the monitor screen. In seconds it would crash into the outpost!

"Brace yourselves!" Tom yelled.

For a split second the craft veered away, but then headed once more for the station. With an earsplitting din of rending metal, the rocket ship plowed into and through the rim of the space wheel! The hoop spun furiously, flinging the crew about like puppets. Stunned, the men were flattened against the compartment's outer bulkhead by the pull of centrifugal force.

Tom clawed his way toward the master control panel. Small reaction jets had been mounted on the wheel after an earlier mishap. He managed to trigger several bursts which slowly braked the wheel to a halt.

"Pete, call Fearing Island!" Tom ordered.

The transmitter was dead, apparently jarred out of commission by the crash. But after minutes of frenzied checking, the trouble was repaired and Tom spoke to the Swifts' rocket base. He directed that the unknown rocket craft be tracked and that his own spaceship, the *Challenger,* be flown up to the space outpost at once.

"Wilco, skipper!" the base operator responded.

While two space medics gave first aid to several of the crew, Tom and Horton surveyed the damage. Three spokes had been smashed and would have to remain sealed off. One was the astronomical observatory.

"Tough break," Horton commented gloomily. "We might have been able to keep the ship in sight by telescope. Our radar got knocked out, too, so the station's practically blind."

"There goes my experiment," Tom said wryly to Bud. The two boys had arrived at the outpost on one of the regular cargo shuttle rockets from Fearing Island. Tom had come to test a new electrostatic-field device in a space environment.

"Did you have time to learn anything?" Bud asked the young inventor.

Tom shrugged. "A little. I was using my new gadget as a wave trap or antenna to capture light of

The rocket ship plowed into the space wheel!

a single wave length from certain stars so I could study their red shift."

"Red shift?" Bud winked at Ken. "What's that —a new Russian football play?"

Tom chuckled. "No, a shift in wave length tells us whether a star is moving toward or away from the sun."

Tom talked with his injured crewmen until the *Challenger* arrived an hour later. This mighty spaceship, in which Tom had outraced foreign cosmonauts to the moon, looked like a huge silver cube caged within circular rails. The rails were tracks for wheeling the ship's repelatron force-ray radiators in any direction to drive the *Challenger* on a specific course.

By this time, a repair crew had retrieved Tom's electrostatic-field device from the astronomy spoke and loaded it into the *Challenger*. Wearing space suits, Tom and Bud boarded the craft.

Hank Sterling, the rugged, blond chief engineer and trouble-shooter of Swift Enterprises, greeted the boys in the ship's flight compartment.

"Any clues yet on the crash, skipper?"

Tom shook his head. "It's a total mystery, Hank, but I'm suspicious it was no accident."

Lights flashed on the element-selector panel as Tom took over the controls. Repulsion beams from the ship's repelatrons speared outward to earth and moon, hurling the *Challenger* forward by reaction. As usual, Bud acted as copilot. He was a flier and astronaut from California, who, like Tom, was eighteen.

"*Challenger* to Fearing," called Tom at the controls. "Give me the latest on that rocket ship."

"Bad news," reported George Dilling, the Swifts' radio chief. "The ship was moving very erratically in a western orbit. Our Pacific tracking station lost contact. But computers indicate that the rocket ship might be descending toward a landing somewhere in Asia."

"Okay. Order all stations to remain alert."

Tom brought the *Challenger* down to ten thousand miles altitude and steered it at meteor speed across the Pacific and Asia. The crew kept a constant lookout by radar, television, and Tom's megascope space prober. There was no sign of the mysterious rocket craft.

At last they headed home to Fearing Island. This strip of land off the Atlantic coast had once been a barren waste of sand dunes and scrubgrass. Now it was a tightly guarded complex of rocket-launching areas and workshops, with fuel tankers and undersea craft berthed at the island's docks.

At Fearing the astronauts debarked, then flew back to Swift Enterprises on the mainland, near the town of Shopton. At this walled four-mile-square experimental station, Tom Swift Jr. and his scientist father worked on their fabulous inventions.

Tom Sr.—a lean, athletic man with keen blue

eyes and close-cropped graying hair—listened to his son's report in the spacious office which they shared in the Main Building.

"Could the rocket ship have burned up in the atmosphere?" Mr. Swift asked.

"It's possible. But it also may have landed at some Asiatic base."

Mr. Swift frowned thoughtfully. "Well, check it out carefully, Tom. Meanwhile, I must fly to Washington tomorrow morning for an urgent conference."

"What about, Dad?" Tom asked eagerly.

The elder scientist said the conference had to do with a probe rocket which the government space agency had fired some time earlier to orbit Mars, but that he had been given no other information. "While I'm gone," Mr. Swift added, "I'd like you to take over my lecture to our latest group of student engineers."

"Okay, Dad. But I don't know how I'll do as a teacher."

"I'm sure you'll keep your students interested," Mr. Swift replied with a twinkle, "even if you don't speak Vishnapurian!"

Swift Enterprises had recently started its own small-scale foreign aid program. Able young scientists from new and underdeveloped countries were being trained in the latest research techniques. The current group had come from Vishnapur, a tiny state north of India, in the foothills of the Himalayas.

Next day Tom prepared to conduct a lecture-demonstration in his private glass-walled laboratory. Bud Barclay watched as the young inventor set up his equipment.

"Going to show them your new electrostatic-field device?" Bud asked.

Tom grinned and nodded. "If I have to make like a prof, I guess I can do it better with one of my own inventions!"

The boys turned as a door burst open. Harlan Ames, Enterprises' tall, dark-haired security chief, came striding in with a piece of paper in his hand. "Tom!" he said. "Take a look at this!"

Tom glanced at the sheet. It bore a message, hand-printed in Oriental-style letters:

THIS IS A FRIENDLY WARNING. FOR YOUR
OWN SAFETY, BE ON GUARD AGAINST THE
STUDENT ENGINEERS FROM VISHNAPUR.
ONE IS A DEADLY SPY AND TRAITOR!

CHAPTER II

ACCIDENTAL BLACKOUT

"DID this warning come through the mail, Harlan?"

"Yes, Tom—postmarked New York City."

"Have you checked with Vishnapur's representative in Washington?" Tom asked.

The security chief nodded. "The official himself got a similar note. He was very much upset—seemed to think the warning may be authentic, since Vishnapur is in a state of political unrest."

Tom recalled that this was one reason why the young engineers, headed by Prince Jahan, the ruler's son, had been sent to America for training. It was hoped that they might modernize their tiny country and thus raise its living standards.

Bud asked, "Did anyone check out these boys before they enrolled at Enterprises?"

"As thoroughly as we could," Ames said.

"Vishnapur is located deep in the Himalayas. Hardly any Westerners are allowed to enter. Our State Department got a rundown on each of the students, but mostly had to take Vishnapur's official word that they were okay."

Tom looked thoughtful. "Harlan, we shouldn't take any hasty action. If we ban the whole group as security risks—especially when one's the son of the Rajah—it could wreck friendly relations between our countries. Let's check into this first."

"But what if one of them *is* a spy?"

"He can't do much more harm if we wait a bit," Tom pointed out. "They've already had the run of the plant for several weeks. As far as my lecture-demonstration goes, I won't be giving away any great secrets."

But Tom did agree that Ames should keep the student engineers under surveillance. "Any leads on that rocket ship?" he added.

"Not yet," Ames said. "Every country with a space program denies the craft was theirs."

Soon afterward, the trainees from Vishnapur filed into Tom's lab. Prince Jahan came first, the others following respectfully. All wore Western-style slacks and sports coats and were bareheaded, except the prince. He always appeared in a white turban, which was studded with a large star sapphire to mark his royal rank.

"*Namaste!*" They smiled at Tom and Bud and made the usual gesture of greeting—bobbing their heads and pressing their palms together with the fingers pointed upward.

Of the eight students, most looked like typical, handsome East Indians, with olive complexions, jet-black hair, and flashing white teeth. But several were almond-eyed, and seemed more Oriental.

Tom took his place at a central workbench and explained that his father could not be present. "I thought you might like to see some experiments I've been working on lately."

A device stood on the bench in front of Tom. It consisted of a round plastic base with slender brass rods sticking up to support two spheres of quartz crystal, one inside the other. Two coils were mounted, one above and one below the crystal globes. From the lower coil, wires were connected to various points on the outer sphere. A thick cable led from the base to a portable electronic console.

"Ah! It will be most rewarding to see the latest invention of the famous Tom Swift Jr.!" said a thick-haired student named Rakshi.

"This isn't an invention yet," Tom said. "I just rigged it up to carry out some experiments in the area of electromagnetic radiation." He explained that he had constructed the device to control and change the shape of electrical fields.

"This is done by the anti-inverse-square-wave technique I developed in making my megascope space prober." Tom said that the technique could focus waves into a beam of constant signal strength, instead of allowing them to radiate outward in all directions.

"Now, I'll demonstrate it," said Tom.

A number of electroscopes were placed about the room. These were glass jars, each with a metal rod passing through its sulphur stopper. Every rod had a metal ball on top and two thin gold leaves hanging at the bottom inside the jar. Tom took a plastic wand with a metal ball on one end and put an electric charge on the ball by touching it to a high-voltage terminal.

"Of course you all know what will happen when I bring this near the electroscopes," he said.

Tom held the wand near the ball of each electroscope in turn. In every one, the gold leaves swung apart as they became similarly charged and repelled each other.

"As you see, the ball has to be very close to the electroscopes because its field is so weak. But now watch what happens when I place the ball inside my field distorter."

Tom separated the crystal globes and inserted the metal ball. Then he twirled several tuning knobs on the console. As he aimed the globes at each electroscope, its leaves swung open!

"Amazing!" Prince Jahan murmured. "Your device has focused and beamed the ball's electrostatic field as far as ten yards."

"Yes, and with a more powerful machine, the range can be almost unlimited," Tom said. He now showed the model he had taken to the space outpost. Its inner sphere contained a mixture of helium, neon, and argon gases and was plated with silvery metal strips. As Tom switched it on, the gas glowed with a bluish-red radiance.

"This model produces its own field, so there's no need to insert a charged object. The inner sphere can be rotated on any axis, making it unnecessary for me to aim the device by hand."

Tom explained that by shaping the electric field into paraboloidal form, he could make use of its ability to reflect electromagnetic radiation and have it serve as an antenna.

The young inventor demonstrated this by turning on a portable TV set. He tuned his device to the proper frequency and the screen promptly went black. When Tom turned off his device, the picture appeared again as clearly as ever.

A student spoke up. "The electric field drew in the whole picture signal so that none was picked up by the TV antenna—is that it?"

"Right," Tom said. "And now for an even more interesting experiment. As you know, white light is made up of a whole spectrum of colors—red, yellow, green, blue, and violet. I'll tune the field to trap light waves of the frequency of green—and watch what happens to the overhead lights."

Everyone stared upward. The lights began to

darken and take on a reddish-purple hue. Suddenly they went out completely! Even the daylight flooding in through the windows faded. In a moment the room was plunged into pitch-blackness except for the glow from the sphere!

"Hey!" Bud cried. "What's happening?"

An alarm siren shrilled across the plant grounds.

Tom worked frantically to correct the trouble as the room filled with a smell of burning insulation. Full light was finally restored.

"I'm afraid my experiment misfired. Instead of trapping light of one wave length, the field pulled in a wide band of frequencies—the whole visible spectrum."

"And in doing so blacked out the whole plant?" Rakshi asked with a supercilious smile.

"Yes, my device absorbed so much energy it burned out the control circuits," Tom admitted. Then he excused himself to answer the ringing phone.

Ames was calling from Enterprises' Security to inquire what had happened. As Tom explained, Ames chuckled.

"Maybe the Defense Department could use that gadget for air-raid blackouts, skipper."

"Very funny. You'd better make an announcement over the PA that everything's okay, Harlan."

The young inventor checked his electrostatic-field device and discovered the trouble had been caused in the laser-driven oscillator circuit.

"I'll have to make the tuning more selective," he explained. "Meantime, class dismissed!"

Prince Jahan said politely, "We thank you, Tom, for this chance to see a great young scientist at work. Please do not feel that your demonstration was a failure."

"Even the—er—accident was most interesting," added a student named Gyong.

As the Vishnapurians filed out, Bud clapped his chum on the back. "If I know Tom Swift, he'll wind up with something twice as good."

Bud watched as the young inventor set to work disassembling his field device. Some time later there was a knock on the door and two pretty girls stepped into the laboratory.

"Well! Sandy and Phyl!" Bud exclaimed.

Sandra Swift, Tom's blond, seventeen-year-old sister, was Bud's favorite date. Her companion, a brunette with sparkling brown eyes, was Phyllis Newton, daughter of Ned Newton, who managed the Swift Construction Company.

"The gate guard told us things were a bit dark around here a while ago," Sandy teased.

Tom grinned good-naturedly. As the girls came into the room, they were all startled by a shrill, high-pitched squeal.

"Are you giving us the razzberry?" Bud asked the girls. His voice seemed to echo queerly.

"No, it's—it's coming from my handbag!" Phyl said in astonishment. She took out a little transistor radio. "Oh! I left this turned on."

Her voice, too, seemed to have an echo—and the echo was coming from the radio! It momentarily shut out the high-pitched squeal.

"Why, you're broadcasting, Phyl!" Sandy laughed.

Tom had already figured out the mystery. "Do you realize what this means?" he said, his eyes sweeping over the laboratory.

"What?" Bud asked, completely baffled.

"There's a transmitter hidden in here!"

At that moment Sandy glanced out the window. Her blue eyes widened. "Look!" she screamed.

CHAPTER III

THE BRONZE BUDDHA

A weird procession of prancing figures was approaching the laboratory building. The creatures had huge, fantastic heads and wore gaudy robes of red, gold, and black.

"They're coming inside!" Phyl gasped.

Soon Tom, Sandy, Bud, and Phyl heard a thunderous pounding on the door. Then it was thrown open and in surged the nightmarish group, playing bells, drums, and cymbals. The crazy din continued as the people capered about the room.

Suddenly Sandy giggled. "It's a masquerade!"

Some of the figures wore grinning, goggle-eyed demon masks, each topped with a ring of tiny skulls. Another had on a deer's head with flowers blooming from its antlers. Two more were giant-headed buffoons—a white-faced woman and a blue-faced, mustachioed man.

At last the wild dance came to a halt and the

figures pulled off their masks. Tom and his companions applauded and cheered. The panting, laughing masqueraders were Prince Jahan and the other students from Vishnapur!

"Terrific!" Tom exclaimed as the dancers bowed.

"It's the most exciting thing I've seen in ages," Sandy declared.

"Then our humble efforts are more than repaid," Jahan said gallantly.

"But what brought this on, if you don't mind my asking?" Bud put in.

The young prince chuckled. "We were celebrating the Festival of Chogyal a bit early."

The Americans looked interested, and Phyl asked, "Who or what is Chogyal?"

"The highest mountain peak in Vishnapur," Jahan replied. "The name Chogyal means 'king' in the various Himalayan dialects, and the festival is held each year in honor of the gods and spirits of the mountain."

Jahan explained that the homesick students had brought the costumes to America, since they would be far from Vishnapur when the festival was celebrated. "It is still more than two weeks away," he added, "but we hoped that a small preview might cheer our young professor."

"Besides," said Rakshi with a grin, "is it not right that the spirits should honor a scientist who can even blot out the daylight?"

Tom took the ribbing good-naturedly and asked what the masks portrayed. The young Asians told him the deer represented a former incarnation of the lord Buddha. The chief demon, black-faced, was called Mahakali. He and his cohorts were made to look as horrible as possible to help the watchers overcome their fear of death.

"And the blue-faced man and white-faced clowns," Prince Jahan added, "are really *acharyas,* or wise men, who keep the demons amused until the good spirits can defeat them."

Sandy and Phyl were already acquainted with Prince Jahan, and Tom now introduced the other students. From their admiring glances, it was clear that the young engineers from Vishnapur found the two American girls very attractive. Bud scowled as Rakshi conversed with Sandy.

"That long-haired creep!" Bud muttered to Tom. "What's he trying to do—beat my time?"

Tom chuckled silently.

"Your country is almost a part of India," Phyl remarked to Prince Jahan, "and yet those aren't Hindu masks, are they?"

"Quite right, Miss Newton. The people of Vishnapur are a mixture. Many, like myself, are Hindus, while others, like my friend Gyong"— Jahan indicated a student with high cheekbones and Oriental features—"are of Tibetan stock. But all celebrate the Festival of Chogyal."

Before leaving, Prince Jahan invited the four teen-agers to dinner at his apartment and promised that the meal would consist of native dishes from his Himalayan homeland.

"Sounds great," said Tom. Bud and the girls also accepted enthusiastically.

After the students had left, Tom glanced around the room. "Now let's find that bug."

"You mean the hidden transmitter?" Sandy asked.

Tom nodded. "Lucky you left your set turned on, Phyl, especially at that frequency. Otherwise, I might never have found out this place was bugged."

Phyl took out the radio again and gave it a puzzled look. "There's no station at this point on the dial," she murmured. "The knob must have twisted when I put the set in my bag."

"No wonder, the way you gals keep your purses crammed!" Bud joked.

"Turn it on again, Phyl," Tom said, "and walk around the lab. The change in volume of the signal may help us locate the transmitter."

Before Phyl could do so, they were all startled by a muffled voice shouting:

"Help! . . . Get me out of here!"

"Good grief!" Sandy exclaimed with a nervous giggle. "Don't tell me you have a prisoner hidden around here, too, Tom!"

The cries for help were repeated. The voice seemed to carry a hollow, tinny echo.

"It's coming from the air-conditioning duct!" Bud said.

"Sounds like Chow!" Tom added, after putting his head close to the louvered outlet.

The boys dashed from the lab and down the hall toward the Swifts' private galley. This was the one-man domain of Chow Winkler, who had been a chuck-wagon cook in Texas. Tom and his father had met him during an atomic research trip in the Southwest. The Swifts had persuaded Chow to become their personal chef at Enterprises and on trips.

The two boys slid to a halt near a janitor's closet as they heard strange noises coming from inside. The door was locked, but Tom opened it with a master key and turned on the closet light. Bud burst into roars of laughter.

Chow's lower half was protruding from an opening in the back wall of the closet. The fat cook was wriggling and kicking his feet furiously.

"For the love of Mike, Chow, what are you doing with your head in that air duct?" Tom exclaimed.

"Never mind the questions, boss! Jest get me out o' this here bear trap afore I turn blue!"

Tom and Bud each took one leg, braced themselves against the closet wall, and began to yank. After much strenuous tugging, there was a *floop!*

"Get me out o' this bear trap!" Chow howled

and Chow Winkler's pudgy figure popped out of the duct opening. The sudden release sent Tom and Bud toppling backward. Tom slammed into some boxes of cleaning compound and Bud knocked loose a mop that was hanging on the wall. The mop flew up and crashed into a shelf laden with soap, pails, and floor wax.

Like a rackety avalanche, the shelf's contents rained down. Chow landed on top of the two boys just in time for a pail to drop squarely over his head.

"Get off us, you blubberhead!" Bud stormed.

"Gimme a chance!" Chow retorted in a smothered voice. Pushed by the two boys, he struggled upright and finally pulled off the pail.

The cook was panting and beet red. His bald dome glistened with perspiration. Tom and Bud were unable to stifle their laughter, but the two girls, who had followed them to the scene, uttered soothing words.

"How did you ever get yourself into such a fix, Chow?" Tom asked.

The accident turned out to have been caused by Tom's blackout. While groping in the dark, Chow had blundered into the closet and the door had slammed shut, locking automatically. Trapped, Chow had recalled seeing an inspection hole to the air duct in the back wall of the closet. He had hoped to squirm through the duct to an adjoining outlet, but in the attempt he had become stuck.

"I felt so blame foolish I kept tryin' to wiggle loose by myself," the Texan confessed, "but finally I jest had to call fer help."

The teen-agers returned to the laboratory. By moving Phyl's radio about and listening as the squeal grew louder or softer, Tom soon located the "bug." The tiny transmitter, an inch square, had been clamped under a metal wall bracket which had served as its antenna.

"One of those students could have planted it during your demonstration," Bud said. "This proves someone in the group is a spy! With this setup, he could tune in on any scientific secrets being discussed in your lab."

Tom frowned thoughtfully. "Perhaps—or for all we know—the bug may have been planted long before today by an Enterprises employee. . . . Well, I'd better turn this transmitter over to Ames and see what he makes of it!"

That evening Tom, Bud, and the girls kept their dinner date with Prince Jahan. The other students had found rooms in a local motel. But Jahan had been ordered by his father, the Rajah, to take separate quarters because of his royal rank.

The prince was enjoying his new-found American freedom and had cooked the dinner himself. The meal began with wheat pancakes, called *chapaties.* This was followed by *kababs,* a highly spiced mutton curry, with rice pilau and two vegetables—*brinjals bhurta,* which was mint-flavored eggplant—and fried *bhindis,* or okra.

The dessert was called *rosagollah.* It consisted of sugar-soaked lumps formed from curdled milk and covered with a thick, saffron-flavored syrup.

"Mmm! Delicious!" Sandy said enthusiastically.

The others agreed, and Bud said, "Your highness, you can really cook!"

The prince beamed. "Please—not 'your highness'—just 'Jahan.' My father would be horrified if he found out, but cooking has always been a hobby of mine."

As they left the table, Jahan said, "And now, I should like to present these two young ladies with small souvenirs from Vishnapur."

He went to a bookshelf and unwrapped a package. As he lifted out a small bronze Buddha figure, Jahan's face took on a puzzled frown. "Strange! I did not order this from the import shop," he murmured. "Oh, well . . . no matter."

He now removed the wrappings from two small figurines—elephants carved from ivory and enameled in gorgeous colors. Each bore a brass howdah.

"How beautiful!" Sandy and Phyl exclaimed as he handed one to each girl.

"They are incense burners," Jahan explained.

At that moment a loud ring announced a caller at the front door of the apartment building. Jahan answered, then pressed the door buzzer so the visitor could enter.

"It is Mr. Ames from your security department, Tom," the prince said, puzzled.

Tom, too, was mystified by the unexpected call. A few moments later Ames entered, accompanied by a tall, well-dressed, dark-complexioned man.

"I'm sorry to intrude," Ames said, "but Mr. Patil Ram, Vishnapur's representative in this country, has received some alarming information which he will pass along."

Mr. Ram bowed stiffly to Jahan. "Your highness, there is a police officer waiting outside. We have a warrant to search your apartment."

Tom, Bud, and the girls gaped in amazement as Mr. Ram explained that the prince was suspected of being a spy and traitor. As Jahan began to protest angrily, Ames's eyes roved about the room. He walked straight to the bronze Buddha figure, picked it up, and removed a rolled-up slip of paper from a hole in the base.

Ames examined the paper. "This is the evidence we're looking for," he said quietly.

CHAPTER IV

A MARTIAN MYSTERY

"WHAT'S this all about?" Tom demanded.

"You'd better see for yourself," Ames replied.

After hastily introducing the Swifts and their friends to the Vishnapur official, he handed the paper to Tom. It bore a printed message:

> PRINCE JAHAN—THE SCIENTIFIC DATA YOU STOLE FROM SWIFT ENTERPRISES HAS BEEN SOLD TO FOREIGN AGENTS FOR A HIGH PRICE. THE GUNS PURCHASED WITH THIS MONEY WILL HELP US OVERTHROW YOUR FATHER, THE RAJAH, AND MAKE YOU OUR NEW RULER. LET US KNOW THE DATE ON WHICH WE ARE TO BEGIN OUR REVOLT.

Tom read the message with a frown. Then Ames passed it on to Mr. Ram.

Jahan's eyes blazed. "Let me see that!"

Mr. Ram showed him the paper. "Preposterous!" Jahan exclaimed. He read the message aloud to Bud and the girls, adding, "No plotter would send such an incriminating note!"

"I agree—the note's silly," Tom said. "If Prince Jahan were guilty, he would already *know* what the guns were for."

Ames nodded. "You have a point there."

"How did Mr. Ram get the tip to come here?"

The official explained that he had received a mysterious telephone call in Washington. The speaker would give no name, but promised to supply an important lead to the traitor if Mr. Ram would come to New York immediately.

"Was the call traced?" Tom asked.

"Yes, to a New York phone booth," Ames said.

"I flew to New York at once," Mr. Ram went on. "A message was waiting for me at the airport. It said that Prince Jahan and his fellow students frequently went to a certain import shop to buy foodstuffs and other items—and that one of them was getting secret messages from Vishnapur concealed inside these goods."

"Is the store in New York?" Tom asked.

"Yes." Mr. Ram named an address in Lower Manhattan. "The airport message also said to check on a small bronze Buddha."

Mr. Ram said he had gone to the shop. Its owner

had looked up his sales records and found that a Buddha figure had been included in an order purchased recently by Jahan.

"But that *proves* Prince Jahan can't be guilty!" Sandy spoke up. "We know he wasn't expecting that bronze Buddha." She told how surprised the prince had been to find it in the package. Phyl and Bud backed her up.

"A clever bit of acting, perhaps."

"What about the language?" Tom put in. "Would a plotter in Vishnapur write to a spy from his own country in English?"

Mr. Ram shrugged. "It is possible. Hindi and various other tongues are spoken in Vishnapur, so English is often used as a common language, just as it is in India."

"I still think the message doesn't ring true," Tom argued. "It gives no real information and it's addressed to Prince Jahan by name—a fatal give-away if the message ever fell into the wrong hands. It even spells out the fact that they're planning to overthrow the Rajah. Apparently some enemy group is trying to frame Prince Jahan!"

Ames and the official looked impressed at Tom's reasoning. Mr. Ram felt, however, that the prince should stand trial in Vishnapur.

"That may be what the plotters want," Ames said. "It would shake people's trust in the royal family and help weaken the government."

"Exactly," Tom agreed. "I think the message

was cooked up right here in America. If one of the students is involved in the scheme, we may be able to catch him. Please wait before you take any action."

Mr. Ram frowned unhappily. "The Rajah is a stern man. If Prince Jahan is guilty and I let him escape, I would be punished severely."

"Then hold him under house arrest for now," Tom suggested. "A police guard can be posted."

Mr. Ram hesitated. "Very well. I shall wait a few days." Turning to Prince Jahan, he added, "I must ask your highness not to leave this apartment. Arrangements will be made to supply you with food and any other needs."

Jahan nodded curtly, then gave Tom a warm handclasp and beamed at Sandy, Phyl, and Bud. "Thank you, my friends, for believing in my innocence. It was fortunate for me that you were here."

Later, as Tom and Bud were driving the girls home, Phyl asked the young inventor, "Do you have any plans for trapping the spy in the group of student engineers?"

"That bug we found may help," Tom replied. He explained that because its broadcasting range was only a few hundred feet, a repeater, or relay transmitter, would have to be planted near the lab. "Ames had the grounds gone over with radio-detection gear, but nothing has turned up—yet."

"Is someone keeping watch?" Sandy asked.

"Yes, around the clock. In fact, I think I'll bunk at the plant tonight in case anything happens. Want to keep me company, Bud?"

"Sure thing!"

Next door to Tom's laboratory was a small apartment. The young inventor often used it when working overtime. After saying good night to the girls, Tom and Bud drove there and went to bed. An alarm buzzer had been rigged so the lookout could signal in case of any suspicious activity. But the night passed without incident.

Mr. Swift arrived from Washington the following day. Bud picked him up at the plant airfield and drove him at once to Tom's lab.

"The conference was even more interesting than I expected, son," the elder scientist reported.

"What was it about, Dad?" Tom asked.

"The news won't be released until noon today, but something has gone wrong with the Mars probe rocket. It won't respond to the radio signal which was to bring it back to earth."

Tom and Bud were amazed, knowing the rocket's electronic gear had been thoroughly tested.

"What a blow to space research!" Tom said. "The instruments aboard must be packed with data on the Martian environment."

"Invaluable," Mr. Swift agreed. "As yet, no one has a clue to what caused the failure."

"Is the rocket still orbiting Mars, Dad?"

"Yes, and it may go on doing so for the next few

hundred years—unless you and I can devise a way to bring it back to earth."

Tom's eyes flashed. "You mean the government is tossing the problem in our laps?"

"Right, son. It should be a real challenge to figure out how to recover a missile from fifty million miles out in space."

"Wow!" Bud exclaimed. "You're not kidding, sir!"

Tom began to pace excitedly. His brain was already at work on the problem. "Dad, you remember how the space agency has often talked about finding a way to retrieve dead satellites and other space junk?"

"Yes. In some cases, the equipment aboard could be used over again and save the government hundreds of thousands of dollars."

"Well, the electrostatic-field device I've been working on may be the answer to both problems! We might even be able to use it to capture the mysterious rocket ship that rammed the outpost, if it ever shows up again!"

While Tom was explaining his idea, an alarm buzzer sounded. It meant that the lookout had spotted a suspect.

Bud darted to the window. "Look!" he hissed. As Tom and Mr. Swift joined him, he pointed to a figure outside.

"Rakshi!" Tom exclaimed.

The student was bending over a clump of

ornamental shrubbery. Tom hastily told his father what had happened while he was away.

"He could be planting that relay transmitter in the bushes right now!" Bud exclaimed.

The boys waited until Rakshi had strolled off, then they rushed out to search among the shrubbery. To their disappointment, there was no sign of any concealed electronic device.

"Have you lost something, my friends?"

Tom and Bud looked up with a start to find Rakshi smiling at them.

"No! We just like to sniff the pretty flowers!" Bud replied.

"Ah, indeed? I paused, myself, just a short time ago to admire the blossoms," Rakshi said. "Rhododendron, I believe, is it not?" The young Asian walked away. The two boys were furious at having been taken unaware by the very person they suspected.

"He sure sneaked up on us," Bud said angrily. "Do you think he knew what we were doing?"

Tom shrugged. "Hard to tell. If Rakshi hid that bug, he knows that once we discover it, we'll be watching for any attempt to plant a repeater. This whole thing could have been a trick to make us tip our hand."

He immediately phoned a report of the incident to Harlan Ames. "By the way, have you checked yet on the East Indian import shop where the bronze Buddha was purchased?"

Ames reported that it was operated by an elderly man named Lal Singh and a clerk, Benny Susak. Neither had a criminal record.

"The plotters must have some connection with that shop," Tom mused. "And they were pretty stupid to give Mr. Ram its name!"

"Right—if the spy message was a frame-up," Ames agreed.

"There must be a link, anyhow," Tom reasoned. "No customer could use that importing setup for transmitting a spy message unless he had someone working in the shop."

"Hmm. That's true," Ames conceded.

"I think Bud and I will pay that place a visit," Tom said.

Late that afternoon the two boys flew to New York City in a Whirling Duck—a VTOL jet plane which Tom had designed. From the heliport they taxied to East Twenty-eight Street and entered the import shop. Its interior was dim and musty. The front section displayed silken saris, rugs, jewelry, and Oriental art objects. Its back wall shelves were piled high with jars and cartons of East Indian foodstuffs, such as ginger, saffron, and spices.

The owner, Mr. Singh, shuffled forward to greet the boys. He was an elderly, dark-skinned man with a kindly face and gentle eyes. Tom explained why they had come and asked if Mr. Singh had waited on Prince Jahan.

"Ah, no. That order was handled by my clerk,

Mr. Susak." He gestured toward his assistant—a thin, sallow-faced young man—who had come out of the back room and was listening closely.

"Could there have been any mistake about that bronze Buddha?" Tom asked the clerk. "The prince claims he never ordered it."

Susak shrugged. "There was no mistake, sir. I remember him picking it out particularly."

Tom asked a few more questions and learned that all goods from India or Vishnapur were obtained from a firm of exporters in Bombay—Mukerji and Sons. Then the boys left.

"That clerk looks like a phony to me," Bud muttered as they walked away.

Tom agreed. "And our visit may worry him. It's almost closing time. Let's see where he goes after work."

After circling the block, Bud found a lookout spot in a dark doorway across the street, next to a dingy movie theater. Tom stationed himself in the alleyway behind the shop. A pile of trash—steel drums and discarded crates—hid him from view.

Presently Susak came out the back door. He glanced around furtively, then hurried off down the alley.

After waiting a moment, Tom started cautiously in pursuit. To his amazement, Susak was already out of sight! Had the clerk slipped into the rear entrance of some other building?

As Tom darted forward to investigate, he passed a small storage shed. A slight noise made him turn his head just as a masked figure, clutching a heavy stick, sprang into view.

Tom tried to duck, but the stick cracked against his skull. With a moan of pain, the young inventor crumpled to the pavement.

CHAPTER V

A HAIR-RAISING
EXPERIMENT

TOM stirred and opened his eyes as consciousness returned. "What happened?" he wondered dully.

A huge gray rat scuttled across his line of vision.

"Ugh!"

Wincing, Tom forced himself to his feet, and rubbed his throbbing head gingerly. He struggled to collect his wits while looking around the alley.

Suddenly he remembered what had happened. "That clerk—Susak! He must have guessed he was being followed and was lying in wait for me!"

Tom was disgusted. The suspect had slipped through his fingers! There was nothing to do but join Bud and go back to Enterprises.

Brushing himself off, Tom strode through the alley and across the street that ran in front of the import shop. He darted to the dark doorway which

Bud had selected for his stakeout—but he was no longer there!

Tom was perplexed. Could Bud have spotted Susak after the man emerged from the alley?

Earlier, the boys had checked the telephone number of a booth in a corner drugstore. It had been agreed that if they became separated one would use the number to call the other.

Tom hurried to the drugstore and waited at the booth. In a few minutes the telephone rang. Tom snatched it off the hook. Bud's voice came over the line.

"Where are you? What happened?" Tom demanded.

"Downtown. Boy, what a relief to hear you answer! You okay?"

Tom told how he had been slugged, then asked Bud for his story.

"While watching the import shop," his friend answered, "I saw a man dart out of the side street to flag a taxi. I realized it was Susak. You didn't seem to be on his trail, so I went after him in another cab."

Bud said the taxi had dropped Susak at a cheap rooming house near Battery Park. "His name's on one of the doorbell cards—Apartment 305."

Tom's brain was working fast. "Bud, I have a hunch Susak panicked when he found out I was following him. So he slugged me to give himself time for a getaway."

"Then why would he risk stopping here?"

"Maybe to clear out some incriminating evidence. Are you sure he didn't spot you?"

"Fairly sure," Bud replied.

"Where are you calling from?"

"A pay phone down the street. I have the rooming house in plain sight."

"Okay. I'll call the FBI and get there fast." Tom jotted down the address and added, "Don't let him get away!"

Bud chuckled. "Leave it to me. I'll slip inside and park near his door."

Tom made a quick call to headquarters, then took a taxi to the street Bud had given him. He got out some distance down the street and started walking back toward the rooming house. Bud was nowhere in sight, so Tom paused in the doorway of a pawnshop.

Three minutes later a black car glided to the curb. A square-shouldered, gray-suited man in a snap-brim hat leaped out and walked over to Tom.

"Martin, FBI," he said, shaking hands. "We can haul Susak in for questioning, but it may be smarter to hold off and see if he leads us to someone else in the spy setup. . . . Where's your friend, by the way?"

"Inside, I think," Tom replied. "Bud was going to keep watch to make sure Susak didn't escape."

"Good. Let's check with him."

Tom and Special Agent Martin strode toward the rooming house, hurried up the steps, and walked in the front entrance. The tenement building was shabby and dirty. A spring lock on the inner door did not work.

"Apparently your chum had no trouble getting in," Martin observed as he pushed the door open.

Inside was a long hallway ending in a flight of stairs. Tom and the FBI agent hurried up the steps and found Bud waiting between the second and third floors. Weird East Indian music reached their ears.

"Susak's in his room," Bud told them. "His phonograph's been going ever since I got here."

Tom was puzzled. If Susak was eager to make a getaway, why would he be lingering in his room? Then a new thought occurred to him.

"Did anyone else arrive here after Susak?"

Bud shook his head. "Nobody except us. Why?"

"There's a wall phone downstairs," Tom replied. "Susak may have called someone—maybe his boss in the spy setup—and now he's waiting for that person to pick him up."

"Good hunch, Tom," said the FBI man.

Hurrying downstairs, Martin roused the landlady—a fat, untidy-looking woman—and learned that Apartment 309 was vacant. The agent arranged for Tom and Bud to hide in this room, then went outside to keep watch from his car.

The boys waited close to the door. Minutes dragged by. Suddenly Tom gasped in dismay.

"What's wrong?" Bud hissed.

"That music! The same piece has played three times—it must be the last record on the stack!"

Bud's face fell. "Good night! You mean Susak's not even in there?"

Tom hurried down to notify Martin. They got a passkey from the landlady, then went upstairs again and knocked on 305. Receiving no answer, the FBI man unlocked the door.

As Tom had feared, the furnished room was vacant! It was clear from the turned-out drawers and general disarray that Susak had made a hasty flight.

"I'll bet he did notice your taxi trailing him, Bud, or else he spotted you after he got here," Tom speculated. "So he put on a stack of records to fool us, and ducked out either by the roof or the rear fire escape."

Both Martin and the boys were chagrined by the suspect's escape. A search of the room failed to turn up any clues. The FBI agent telephoned the police, requesting that all scout cars be on the lookout for the fugitive. Then he drove Tom and Bud to the heliport and they returned to Shopton.

Next day the young inventor plunged into work on his idea for retrieving objects in space. Bud dropped by the laboratory to watch the experiment. Tom was just switching off a vacuum pump connected to a thick-walled glass chamber. Inside the airless chamber, a metal-plated ping-pong ball hung from a nylon cord.

"What's this—a new game?" Bud asked.

Tom chuckled. "No, a demonstration of how I hope to bring back that Mars probe rocket."

"Hmm. Give me the low-down, prof."

"Well, let's pretend that the ping-pong ball is the rocket," Tom began. He switched on his newly repaired electrostatic-field device and trained the inner crystal globe toward the glass chamber.

Instantly the ball swung toward Tom!

"Say, that's neat, boy. How does it work—by magnetic attraction?"

"No, you might say it turns the ping-pong ball into an electron-drive engine." When Bud looked blank, Tom explained that the field beamed out by his device, in effect, polarized the ping-pong ball, making its front side highly positive.

"Sort of a polar-ray beam, eh?"

"You could call it that, I guess. Anyhow, the electrons in the metal coating, being negative, are driven toward the rear side. And since the ball is in a vacuum, the electrons jet out freely at high velocity."

"I get it!" Bud exclaimed. "The ball is driven forward by reaction—just like a jet-propelled plane or a rocket!"

"Exactly," Tom said with a nod. "And if I can beam out a powerful enough field—"

He was interrupted by a knock at the door. "Come in!" Tom called.

Rakshi entered the lab. "I trust I am not intruding," he said smoothly. Without waiting for a reply, he walked into the room, his eyes flickering over the experimental apparatus.

"What is it you wanted?" Tom asked curtly.

Rakshi's face took on a worried look. "As loyal friends of Prince Jahan, the other trainees and myself are most perturbed that he is suspected of wrongdoing. Can you tell us if he will be cleared soon of these false charges?"

"That's up to your own government," Tom said. "Personally, I don't believe he's guilty."

"Ah! That is good news indeed!" Rakshi brightened and peered inquisitively at the glass-walled vacuum chamber. "May I ask what sort of research you are engaged in?"

Tom winked at Bud. "I'll show you," Tom told the student. "But first you'd better step on that rubber mat to avoid any danger of shock."

Rakshi did so. Tom swiveled the inner crystal globe slightly, then switched on his static-field device. Rakshi let out a startled shriek. *His long, wavy, carefully combed hair was standing on end—sticking out in all directions!*

Bud was choking with laughter. Rakshi spluttered angrily, red-faced with rage.

"Sorry," Tom said, switching off his machine. "I'm afraid I didn't have the field aimed quite

Rakshi let out a startled shriek

right so I—er—accidentally electrified your hair. If you'll wait till I readjust the field focus, I'll demonstrate—"

"Do not bother!" Rakshi snapped. Combing his hair furiously, he stalked out of the lab.

Bud laughed till his sides ached. "I'll bet that's the last time he comes snooping around here!"

"We hope." Tom grinned.

He continued working on his device. First he altered the amplifying circuits to make the field more powerful, then constructed a repelatron "catcher." This catcher would brake the speed of the rocket or other object being retrieved, in order to keep it from crashing into the operator's spacecraft.

"All set," Tom said finally.

On Saturday morning he and Bud flew to Fearing Island and took off in the *Challenger* with a small crew to test the invention.

As soon as the huge spaceship was above the atmosphere, a small missile was launched. Then Tom and Bud donned space suits and went outside to the landing platform where the static-field machine and repelatron catcher had been set up.

Tom switched on the machine and beamed out a field toward the speeding missile. By now, it had dwindled to a glittering speck in the blue-black space void.

The invisible electric field enveloped the

rocket. In seconds it lost its forward momentum and began to move back toward the *Challenger.* Faster and faster it came, retracing its original flight path.

The boys were startled as the missile became more visible. Instead of moving on a straight course, it was fluttering and zigzagging!

"Hey! What's wrong with it?" Bud exclaimed.

"I don't know . . . I can't imagine." Tom was baffled by the rocket's curious, jerky motion. He studied the dials of his control console and made several adjustments.

By now, the missile was hurtling toward their ship at terrific velocity.

"Why isn't it slowing down, skipper? That thing's getting too close for comfort!"

Tom gasped. "Good grief! The repelatron catcher's not braking it!" He tinkered hastily with the repulsion-ray device but could not locate the trouble. "The repelatron must be off frequency, Bud!" Tom cried out. "Its rays are having no effect!"

In a moment the missile would crash into the *Challenger!*

CHAPTER VI

THE SAFFRON CLUE

"HANK!" Tom shouted into his helmet microphone. "Stop the missile! Use the ship's repelatrons!"

The *Challenger* gave a backward lurch as its rays stabbed out against the onrushing rocket. Tom and Bud clung to the nearest supports. A split second later the missile came to a shuddering halt—its skin glowing cherry red from the sudden dissipation of energy.

"Whew!" Bud said shakily. "I expected us all to get knocked galley west!"

"We would have," Tom said, "if Hank hadn't braced the ship beforehand. He was using beams aimed against the earth and moon to cushion the shock of catching the rocket."

After mooring the rocket, Tom and Bud went back up to the flight compartment and removed their space helmets. Hank Sterling was at the controls.

"Neat catch, Hank," Tom said.

"Sure glad I didn't miss," the engineer joked. "That rocket was almost down our throats."

Tom grinned dryly. "The repelatron catcher goofed off at the wrong time."

Bud gave his chum an encouraging pat. "You proved your machine could reel in that rocket, even if it did wobble a bit en route."

"Wobble is right!" Tom agreed. "I'll have to find out what caused that and fix it—and also iron out the bugs in the repelatron catcher."

After returning to Enterprises, the young inventor worked for the rest of the afternoon in his laboratory. That evening he gave a full report to his father. "The repelatron catcher will have to be shielded with Tomasite," he added. "I found out that induction currents were throwing the repulsion off frequency."

"What about the missile's zigzag motion?"

"That's not so much of a problem as I thought, Dad. In generating the field, we were producing pulses instead of delivering a steady output, but I can fix that with a bit more work on the filter circuits."

"Very good. Then you think your machine can handle our government assignment?" Mr. Swift asked.

Tom nodded eagerly. "With a larger, more powerful model, I'm sure I can bring back the Mars probe rocket. And I'd like to design a special spacecraft to carry the machine. After we wind up this project, the government can use it for regular space salvage work."

Tom sketched his ideas for the vehicle.

Mr. Swift was enthusiastic. "Get right to work on it Monday," he advised. "Uncle Ned can iron out the contract details with the government space agency."

On Monday morning, however, Tom received an urgent call from Harlan Ames. "The police have found that clerk from the import shop," the security chief told him.

"Benny Susak?" Tom asked excitedly.

"Right. But his capture may not help us much. He was hit by a car and so far hasn't been able to answer any questions."

Ames explained that a policeman had spotted a man trying to break into the shop the night before. The officer had gone after the intruder, who had fled despite a warning shot fired over his head. The man had darted across the street in front of a moving car and been struck down.

"He was rushed to a hospital," Ames went on, "and later the police identified him as Susak. He's in critical condition, so if we hope to talk to him we'd better get over there fast."

Tom and Ames took off for New York City, and after landing, taxied to the hospital. A police lieutenant met them outside Susak's room.

"You got here at just the right time," Lieutenant Murchison said. "Susak looks as if he's coming to."

They found the young man, swathed in bandages, moaning slightly. A doctor and a nurse stood at his bedside.

Presently Susak's lips moved, but only a faint, mumbling sound came from them. Tom thought he caught the word "saffron" several times.

"That was it, all right—saffron," Lieutenant Murchison agreed. "But what's he trying to say?"

The injured man's face bore a desperate look and perspiration beaded his forehead. A few minutes later he lapsed into unconsciousness. The doctor checked Susak's pulse and examined his eyes, then looked up with a shrug.

"I'm afraid that's all you're likely to get out of him, gentlemen. He's in a deep coma."

As Tom left the room with Ames and Murchison, he was frowning. "I have a hunch Susak went back to the shop to get something vitally important—something that might incriminate him even worse or give away the whole plot."

"Why wait three days to go after it?" Ames objected. "He made his getaway Thursday."

"I think I can explain the time lapse," the officer put in. "The owner, Lal Singh, lives in back of the shop. Susak probably didn't dare break in while Singh was on the premises. But last night he was out."

Ames nodded. "What about 'saffron'?"

"Saffron's used in East Indian cooking," Tom said. "I tasted it in a dessert when we had dinner at Prince Jahan's. There's probably some in the shop and it may be connected with whatever Susak was mumbling about."

"Let's check it out," Lieutenant Murchison said.

All three drove to the import shop in the police officer's car. Mr. Singh had just opened the store.

"Saffron?" the elderly shopkeeper murmured. "Yes, we carry that." He seemed puzzled, but led the way to the shelves at the rear and pointed to an array of jars and small baled packages of the yellow substance.

"May we examine your stock?" Tom asked.

"By all means!" Singh gestured politely.

Tom ferreted among the containers. A moment later he gave a cry of triumph and pulled out a notebook from behind the jars.

"This yours?" Murchison asked the shop-keeper.

"No, no." Singh seemed to be amazed. "My clerk Susak kept the shelves filled. He must have placed it there."

The three examined the notebook eagerly.

"You really struck gold, skipper!" Ames exclaimed. "This is a code book!"

Its pages bore lists of merchandise items and business phrases with a code meaning for each. The book also contained instructions for invisibleink messages on invoices, purchase orders, and bills of lading.

Two slips of paper were tucked in the back of the notebook—apparently copies of recent messages, jotted down by Susak. One ordered the clerk to frame Prince Jahan by planting a fake note in the hollow bronze Buddha, which Susak was to wrap up with the prince's next purchase. The other message read:

SWIFTS TO RETRIEVE MARS ROCKET. TS
WORKING ON NEW INVENTION TO DO THIS.
WARN HIMALAYAS HE WILL ALSO USE IT
TO CAPTURE SHIP IF SIGHTED.

SNOWMAN

Tom, Ames, and Lieutenant Murchison hurried to police headquarters to go over the book more carefully.

" 'Snowman' must be a code name of the spy at Enterprises," Ames deduced. "Maybe Rakshi! Tom, could he have been eavesdropping outside your lab when the lookout spotted him?"

"He may have been trying to with a pocket receiver—but the bug was already switched off," Tom replied. "Anyhow, there was an announcement about the rocket over the noon newscasts that day. And within an hour word got all over Enterprises that I was going to adapt my new invention for the retrieval job."

"What about the warning that you'll use your invention 'to capture ship if sighted'?" Ames asked. "I take it that refers to the rocket ship that crashed into the space outpost?"

Tom nodded. "I'm afraid there was talk around the plant about that, too. But this proves there *is* a spy at Enterprises—probably among the trainees!"

Ames informed Tom that the Vishnapurians were being kept under close watch. Lieutenant Murchison suggested that all the records and correspondence at Singh's shop be checked to see if any earlier code messages could be found.

"Good idea," Ames said.

As Tom flew back to Shopton, he kept turning the mystery over and over in his mind. What was behind the sinister spy plot? And how did the weird yellow rocket ship tie in?

That afternoon, as Tom was busy in his lab, he had an unexpected visitor—Prince Jahan.

"I have been completely cleared, thanks to you, my friend!" Jahan announced joyfully. "And now there is one more favor I wish to ask. You and Bud, and Sandy and Phyl, must cancel all your plans, starting a week from today."

"How come?" Tom asked with a surprised grin.

"Because you will be flying to Vishnapur with me and my fellow students—as palace guests for the great summer Festival of Chogyal!"

CHAPTER VII

THE GODDESS OF DOOM

TOM was taken aback by the unexpected invitation. "That sounds great," he said. "But I'm afraid I won't be able to get away."

Jahan's handsome face clouded. "You must, Tom!" he pleaded. "Now that you have lifted the shadow of suspicion from my head, my friends and I have made special plans to return home and celebrate! Can you not take a short vacation and join us?"

"But Vishnapur's halfway around the world. And honestly, Jahan, this Mars rocket job may—"

Suddenly the young inventor paused as a thought came to him. He rubbed his jaw thoughtfully. "How long does the festival last?"

"For a week everyone in Vishnapur does homage to Chogyal with dancing, feasting, and merrymaking," Jahan replied. "A week you will never forget! . . . Please come, Tom."

"Okay—gladly—if I can arrange things with my father. And if Bud and the girls agree to go."

Jahan beamed. "I shall count on you all!"

When Bud heard the news he eagerly accepted. That evening Tom broached the matter to his father.

"The technical problems connected with my rocket retriever are all licked now," the young inventor reported. "Our spacecraft to carry the machine will be a cinch. Its repelatron drive will be the same as the propulsion system in the *Challenger*—in fact simpler, since the ship itself will be much smaller."

"The basic conformation is all worked out?"

"Right, Dad. I can start mocking-up the fuselage tomorrow with Arv, and I'll ask Hank to assign the systems engineers. Art Wiltessa can follow through on my static-field device."

Mr. Swift considered a moment. "Then you can have the project well under way by the end of the week?"

Tom nodded eagerly. "Yes, but it will need supervision while I'm gone—*if* I go, that is. Could you possibly find time to handle it?"

Sandy, who was perched on the arm of her father's easy chair, wheedled, "Just think—we're invited as palace guests! A chance of a lifetime to enjoy a week of Oriental luxury!"

Mr. Swift chuckled. "When you put it that way, my dear, how can I refuse? . . . Anyhow, son, this Mars rocket project is my responsibility, too, and I can wind up my bionics experiments soon. So the answer is Yes."

Mrs. Swift readily gave permission for the trip, then Sandy telephoned Phyllis Newton. Phyl at once consulted her parents, and the Newtons, too, gave their consent.

Next day, at the experimental station, Tom explained the trip to Harlan Ames and added, "Spending a week with those trainees may give me a chance to spot the real spy. What's more, that Snowman message indicates to me that the rocket ship is based in the Himalayas. Touring Vishnapur, I may be able to pick up a real lead!"

Ames agreed but warned, "The whole Himalayan frontier is an international trouble spot, skipper. So watch your step."

Tom promised to be cautious on any flights over the rugged mountain chain.

The next few days were spent in frenzied activity. Tom worked long hours and twice slept overnight at the plant. But after a restful weekend, he was fresh and eager for the trip.

Late Sunday evening the *Sky Queen* took off. Included in Tom's party were Chow and several crewmen. Prince Jahan and the other trainees were delighted at the chance to ride in the huge, atomic-powered Flying Lab.

"I have to stop off in Bombay on some company business," Tom told Jahan as they streaked across the moonlit Atlantic into the westward-sweeping dawn. "Perhaps you and some of the other students would escort the girls around the city while Bud and I do our errand."

"We shall be delighted to do so!" Jahan said.

After the prince had left the flight compartment, Bud asked, "What's this errand?"

"Remember Mr. Singh telling us that he gets all his Indian and Vishnapurian goods from Mukerji and Sons in Bombay?" When Bud nodded, Tom continued. "I'd like to visit that outfit and see if we can pick up any clues on how those spy messages were transmitted."

"Smart idea! Let's give it a try."

At supersonic speed the flight took just over three hours. It was midmorning in Bombay as the plane swooped down over the mud-brown Arabian Sea. They landed at Santa Cruz Airport on the outskirts of India's bustling west coast metropolis.

After clearing customs, Tom inquired about the firm's address, which was on Dadhabai Naoroji Road near the waterfront. He and Bud took a taxi into the city.

"Did you notice Rakshi putting on that big-shot act for the girls?" Bud grumbled as they sped along a wide, modern expressway.

Tom grinned. "Relax, pal. They'll be too busy seeing the sights to fall for his line."

Part of the route into the city led through grimy

factory and tenement districts. When they approached the heart of Bombay's business section, however, the boys were thrilled by its skyline of office buildings and modern, glass-tiered apartments along the wide palm-fringed avenues. Red double-decker buses and sleek sports cars jockeyed their way through the heavy traffic.

The taxi stopped at a building labeled MUKERJI AND SONS. The establishment seemed to be both a store and a warehouse. Entering, Tom and Bud walked up to a counter heaped with merchandise. A *babu,* or clerk, in a high-collared white coat and a *dhoti* came forward.

"May I help you, sirs?"

Tom pretended they were tourists on a shopping tour of Bombay. He chatted with the clerk and mentioned the import shop in New York. "Mr. Singh told us he obtains his goods from your firm," Tom went on, "so we thought we'd stop in and look around."

A stout man in a business suit had come out from the stacked aisles behind the counter. He beamed at the boys. "Mr. Singh is a good customer of ours. I am most happy to have you visit us. Permit me to introduce myself—Ved Mukerji, the present owner of this firm."

Tom introduced Bud and added, "I'm Tom Swift."

"Not the famous young inventor?" Mr. Mukerji exclaimed. "This is indeed an honor!"

The stout man insisted upon showing the two boys over his entire establishment. The back of the building was used as warehouse space. On the upper floor, clerks were busy checking goods from all over Asia, while in the office three young Indian women, clad in graceful flowing saris, were engaged in filing and typing. Tom found it hard to believe that any of the three could be connected with the spy plot.

Before leaving, Tom bought several shawls from Kashmir and some silver cuff links as take-home gifts. Bud plucked a curious-looking pin off the counter. "I'll bet Sandy would go for this!"

The pin was of black onyx carved in the likeness of a four-armed woman wearing a necklace of skulls. Her eyes were tiny red rubies.

Tom grinned. "Unusual—but a bit gruesome."

"Nahin! Ise mat chhuo—No! Do not touch this!" The clerk darted forward and tried to take the pin, but Bud held on to it. "What's the matter? Isn't it for sale?"

"Certainly you may buy it," said Mr. Mukerji. He spoke sharply in Hindi to the clerk, then turned back to the boys. "The pin arrived in a shipment from Vishnapur, and Chandra here— my chief clerk—rudely wished to keep it for himself."

Bud offered to forego the purchase, but Mr. Mukerji insisted he take the pin and named a low

The clerk tried to take the pin away from Bud

price. "The carved figure is Kali, the Hindu goddess of death," Mr. Mukerji explained. "My clerk may have feared the pin would bring you bad luck. No doubt that was the true reason for his concern—was it not, Chandra?" The clerk shrugged sullenly.

After leaving, Tom and Bud taxied along the scenic Marine Drive, then up past beautiful hanging gardens to the top of Malabar Hill. With Chowpatty Beach spread out below, the boys had a breath-taking view of the seaside city.

It was now almost noon, so the boys had the taximan take them to the Taj Mahal Hotel overlooking the water, where they were to meet the others for lunch. Nearby stood an imposing arch which the driver said was called the Gateway to India.

Tom and Bud waited in the hotel lounge. The two girls soon arrived, escorted by Prince Jahan and three other young engineers from Vishnapur, including Rakshi. Sandy was delighted with the Kali pin, but Rakshi gave Bud an angry glare.

"It is not at all a becoming pin for a beautiful American girl to wear," he muttered.

"I think it's wonderful!" Sandy said, pinning it to her dress.

Over lunch, the girls told how they had watched an Indian movie scene being filmed.

"We found out that Bombay produces even more motion pictures than Hollywood does," Phyl added.

Suddenly Tom's pencil radio buzzed. It was a call from the *Sky Queen*. The plane's radioman reported that the American consulate wanted Tom, Bud, and the whole group of Enterprises trainees to pay a good-will visit to a technical school in Bombay at two o'clock that afternoon. Reporters and news photographers would be on hand.

Tom groaned. "I suppose word of our arrival leaked out at the airport."

Jahan's eyes twinkled. "As a prince I am not bound by the usual rules, Tom. So please extend my regrets and say that I had a prior engagement—as guide for two young ladies."

The girls were delighted to have company for the afternoon.

"Let's visit those cave temples at Elephanta we've heard so much about," Phyl suggested.

Sandy and the prince readily agreed. After saying good-by to Tom and the others, the trio taxied to the ferry landing where they boarded a motor launch for the island of Elephanta, six miles across the harbor.

The beautiful little island had two long hills with a valley between. Picnickers were lounging among the trees. The girls and Prince Jahan accompanied other tourists from the landing stage to the main cave, Ganesh Gupha. It had been excavated in a terrace of rock. Wide steps, flanked by stone elephants, led up to the temple entrance.

Inside, Sandy and Phyl were struck with awe by the huge sculptures of Indian gods and goddesses. Most imposing of all was the Trimurti—a three-headed figure of Siva, Vishnu, and Brahma, carved from living rock.

"It's almost spooky!" Phyl murmured.

Other sightseers were milling about as they came out of the temple. Suddenly Sandy gave a little scream. "That man! . . . He snatched my Kali pin!" She pointed to a turbaned, bearded figure dashing down the temple steps.

Prince Jahan darted in pursuit, as the thief fled among the trees and up the hillside. He was poorly dressed in a ragged, high-collared *achkan* and *dhoti*. Cresting the hill, he headed down toward the opposite shore of the island. Jahan was twenty yards behind.

As the man neared the beach, he waved his arms frantically. A speedboat which had been circling offshore streaked toward the island.

Jahan reached the man and seized him by the shoulder. The thief whirled and aimed a vicious punch at the prince. Jahan blocked the blow and struggled to wrest the pin from the man's hand. A moment later the speedboat reached shore and three men, armed with daggers, sprang out!

CHAPTER VIII

A ROYAL WELCOME

AS the three thugs from the boat rushed toward him, Jahan turned to meet their attack. The bearded thief seized his chance and felled Jahan with a blow to the head.

Meanwhile, Sandy's and Phyl's cries had roused the other sightseers. One man, an American tourist, raced over the hill and down to the beach as Jahan was struggling to his feet.

By this time, the thief and his confederates had started toward the boat. Jahan lunged after them and grabbed one by the leg. The thug turned, his dagger raised, ready to strike.

Scarcely pausing, the tourist scooped up a rock and hurled it at the knife wielder. It hit him on the temple, knocking him to the ground before the dagger could strike. The bearded thief viciously kicked Jahan out of the way while the other two thugs dragged their stunned companion into the boat and hopped aboard. Then the pilot gunned it and roared out to sea.

Prince Jahan was in a dazed state when the tourist reached him. The young man shook his head to clear his brain as the man helped him up. "Feel all right?"

"Yes, thank you. Was it you who threw the stone?"

"A lucky hit. I'm glad it dropped him before he could knife you." The American was tall and sinewy-looking, with a thick brown mustache. He wore a straw hat, dark glasses, and a white suit. A camera was slung around his neck.

"You saved my life, sir," Jahan said warmly.

"Forget it. My name's Hugh Mortlake."

"And I am Prince Jahan of Vishnapur."

The American looked startled. Sandy and Phyl came hurrying toward them, accompanied by several more sightseers. By this time the speedboat was far out. Since there was no telephone on the island, there seemed to be no chance of intercepting the criminals.

"They were obviously *dacoits*," said one Indian man. He explained to the girls that dacoits were murderous thugs who operated in gangs.

"I'm afraid I failed to get back your Kali pin, Sandy," Prince Jahan apologized.

"You were brave to go after that thief!"

As the group started back to the ferry landing, Jahan introduced Hugh Mortlake to the girls.

The American said he was an archaeologist and had come to India to collect ancient art objects for the Vroom Museum in Philadelphia.

"I wish there were some way to show my gratitude to you, Mr. Mortlake," Jahan said.

The man gave him a thoughtful glance. "As a matter of fact, there is."

"Please name it."

"Vishnapur has been shut off from the world behind its mountains for hundreds of years. Your country allows few foreigners to enter."

Jahan nodded regretfully. "I am trying to persuade my father to change all that."

"I was hoping to go there," Mortlake went on, "to investigate the ancient ruins at Shankaru. But your authorities refused to grant me a visa to enter."

"You have certainly earned the right to visit Vishnapur," said Jahan. "Can you be ready to leave this afternoon?"

"Just give me time to get my luggage."

After returning to Bombay on the ferry, the four reported the theft to the police. Then Jahan and the girls accompanied Mortlake to his hotel and afterward taxied to the airport.

Tom's group was already aboard the *Sky Queen*, ready to take off. After hearing what had happened at Elephanta, the young inventor welcomed Mortlake as a passenger on the Flying Lab.

As they winged north from Bombay, Bud noticed Tom had become silent and thoughtful. "What's going on in that high-powered brain of yours?" he asked.

"Bud, I can't help thinking there's more to the theft of that Kali pin than meets the eye."

"How so?" the copilot inquired.

"Well, those three thugs didn't just *happen* to be cruising offshore. The whole thing must have been planned beforehand."

Bud agreed and added, "Sandy says she saw that bearded guy on the ferry going over."

"Which means he may have been following her."

"Just to snatch the pin?" Bud frowned. "How can you be sure? That dacoit gang may make a regular habit of robbing tourists."

"Maybe," Tom conceded. "But it still strikes me as more than a chance theft—especially with Mortlake showing up so conveniently."

"You think *he* may have been part of the plot?"

Tom looked worried. "Ever since Mortlake came aboard, I've had a feeling I'd seen him before. It just came to me where—sitting near us at lunch in the hotel."

Bud whistled. "Then he may have heard the girls talking about the trip to Elephanta. That would have given him time to cook up the theft!"

"Exactly. And Jahan, being Sandy's escort, was almost certain to go after the thief—giving Mortlake a chance to save his life and wangle an invitation to fly to Vishnapur with us."

"Wow!" Bud was impressed by Tom's reasoning. "Maybe we'd better keep an eye on Mr. Mortlake."

Flying over the hazy blue mountains beyond Bombay, they streaked across the great Indian subcontinent and finally passed over the Ganges River. Soon the green foothills and snowy peaks of the Himalayas loomed in the distance.

A land of steep gorges, emerald valleys, and rocky uplands came into view as the Flying Lab zoomed out of the clouds toward the capital city of Chullagar. Tom had radioed ahead that they would land shortly before five o'clock.

The raw dirt airfield lay just outside the city. As the *Sky Queen* touched down, Tom glimpsed two outmoded twin-engine planes in a wooden hangar. Jahan said these were the Rajah's aircraft. A helicopter also stood on the field. "That belongs to my uncle, Prince Gopal, who is a skilled pilot," Jahan added.

As the passengers disembarked, a smiling, turbaned man with a twirled mustache came out to greet them. He was followed by several aides. Jahan introduced the man as Prince Gopal, the Rajah's *dewan,* or chief minister.

"Welcome to Vishnapur!" Gopal exclaimed. He shook hands Western style with the boys and Mortlake, and bowed gracefully to kiss Sandy's and Phyl's hands. "The Rajah has sent his own royal beasts to bear you to the palace," he said.

A dozen elephants with canopied howdahs on their backs were standing in line nearby.

Prince Jahan and Sandy rode in the two-seat howdah atop the first elephant, followed by Gopal and Phyl on the next, then Tom and Bud. After them came Mortlake, Tom's crew, and Jahan's fellow trainees.

Chow Winkler seemed somewhat leery getting into his howdah. Tom grinned as the cook waddled up the elephant's trunk and over its head, assisted by the *mahout,* or driver. But Tom noticed that once aboard he seemed to enjoy himself hugely.

The route to the palace led over mud and cobbled streets, past buildings topped by layer upon layer of pagoda-style roofs. Smiling people lined the streets, cheering Prince Jahan and his guests. The Americans smiled, but the pitching, heaving backs of the elephants shook them up considerably.

"This is worse than a bucking bronco!" Bud groaned. "A guy could get seasick on these!"

The palace, topped by domes, rose many stories high, its rose-colored façade pierced by rows of carved lattice windows.

Servants led the party into a tapestried drawing room strewn with exquisite Oriental rugs. Here they were presented to His Highness Rajah

Krishna Baragyal II, his Rani, or Queen—Jahan's stepmother—and their court.

The Rajah, a gray-bearded, dignified man, received his guests graciously, but his stern manner somewhat overawed them.

"Don't let him scare you," Jahan whispered, grinning. "He's a kindhearted old tyrant."

The Rani and her court ladies wore silken saris, gold bangles, and embroidered lace shawls. Tom saw them darting jealous glances at the two attractive American girls.

Once in their rooms, Phyl murmured in dismay, "Those court ladies resent us!"

"I'm afraid you're right," Sandy agreed, laughing. Suddenly her blue eyes twinkled. Sending for her brother, Sandy handed him the girls' only can of hair spray. "Please, Mr. Genius, can you whip us up a couple of gallons of this?"

"Sure, I guess so," Tom said, puzzled. "Why?"

"There's no time to explain. Oh, and could you make something to spray it on with?"

"Would a paint spray gun do?"

"Wonderful! But please hurry!"

Tom and Bud sped back to the *Sky Queen* in a royal jeep. Bud was convulsed with laughter as Tom analyzed the hair spray and began to concoct a batch. "Quiet, or I'll beautify *you* with this stuff!" Tom retorted.

In an hour the boys were back at the palace. The court dinner and reception had been scheduled for eight-thirty. But a servant announced that it would be delayed.

Prince Gopal chuckled. "I suspect that Miss Swift and Miss Newton have caused quite a dither among our court ladies!"

When the reception finally got under way, Tom and Bud gaped. The court ladies, beaming with pride, had their long, jet-black hair done in fashionable American styles. The Rani and her chief lady-in-waiting were wearing dresses of Sandy's and Phyl's let out at the seams. The others had on hastily sewn-together copies.

The two American girls, however, wore Indian saris and gold bangles with a *tikka,* or beauty spot, above their eyes!

"Sandy and Phyl are *still* the belles of the ball!" Prince Jahan confided with a chuckle.

Later, Prince Gopal drew Tom aside. The dewan's face was serious. "How much do you know about this man Mortlake?" he questioned.

Tom shrugged. "Only what he says—that he is an archaeologist for an American museum. Why?"

"It is against the law to remove ancient art objects from Vishnapur," Gopal went on. "I suspect that is Mortlake's real purpose. As chief of his highness's security police I had his luggage searched. This was found inside."

Tom gasped as Prince Gopal held out a tiny, gleaming black figure with twin ruby eyes. *It looked exactly like Sandy's stolen Kali pin!*

CHAPTER IX

THE POISON LAKE

IT seemed too great a coincidence, Tom thought, that Mortlake would have a duplicate of Sandy's pin. This looked like the same one!

"Have you heard what happened at Elephanta?" Tom asked the dewan.

Prince Gopal nodded grimly. "Was the Kali pin which was snatched from your sister similar to this one?"

"Just like it."

"Then no doubt we believe the same thing—that Mortlake hired dacoits to steal the pin."

Tom was amazed by this remark. He had assumed that if Mortlake had faked the robbery, it was to provide an excuse for rescuing Jahan and winning permission to enter Vishnapur. "Is the pin valuable enough for Mortlake to want to steal it?"

"Definitely!" Gopal said. "I have had the pin

examined by one of our historical experts. He has identified it as a relic from Shankaru."

"Shankaru?" Tom exclaimed. "That's the place Mortlake is hoping to visit! What's so important about it?"

Gopal explained that centuries ago, a rich civilization had existed in Vishnapur. This was before her present people had migrated into the mountain valleys from India and Tibet. The ancient craftsmen had turned out exquisite works of art. "The black onyx Kali figure is only a sample," he explained. The civilization had died out in the mists of history. Now, the only trace left was a heap of ruins at a site called Shankaru several days' journey north from Chullagar.

"The few relics of this civilization are now almost priceless," Prince Gopal stated. "That is why none may be taken out of the country. Museums and collectors would give a great deal for an item like this pin."

Tom mulled over the information. "There's no way to prove this is my sister's pin."

"That is true," Gopal conceded. "And since Mortlake is an honored guest of the Rajah, I shall take no steps against him. But it is clear the man may be a thief."

Prince Gopal also asked Tom to say nothing about the matter to Jahan or the Rajah—at least until he had had time to investigate further and find out how the pin had been purloined from

Vishnapur. "It might cause trouble," he added wryly, "if they were to learn their police had allowed such a relic to be smuggled all the way to Bombay!"

Prince Gopal then took out a beautiful emerald ring, flashing with green fire, and handed it to Tom. "Since I cannot return the Kali pin to your sister, please give her this."

After the dinner party, Tom gave Sandy the ring and explained the situation. She was thrilled with the gift, but her brother was still troubled by what had happened. If Mortlake was a thief, Tom wanted nothing more to do with him. Could it be, however, that the dacoits or smugglers had planted the pin in Mortlake's luggage for some reason?

After mulling over the problem, Tom decided to give the man a chance to speak for himself. He went to the archaeologist's room and knocked on his door. Mortlake opened it, surprised. "What brings you here, Tom?"

"It's a delicate subject, and I don't know how to begin," Tom replied as Mortlake motioned him to a chair.

"How delicate?"

"Personal. To do with you and an ugly rumor."

Mortlake's face clouded, but Tom could detect no look of guilt. "Okay, out with it, Tom."

As diplomatically as possible, Tom told Mortlake about the stolen article which reportedly had been found in the baggage. Before he could continue, Mortlake, red in the face, cried out, "It's a lie! If anything was there, someone put it there to incriminate me—and by heavens I'll find out who it was!"

"Hold it! Just cool down a minute," Tom said as Mortlake was about to yank the bell cord for a servant. The man seemed so honestly enraged that Tom was inclined to believe his innocence.

The archaeologist stood lost in thought a moment, then asked, "What did they find?"

When Tom told him, Mortlake was astounded. "I swear I know nothing about your sister's Kali pin!"

He seemed even more startled when Tom told him the onyx ornament had come from Shankaru. But he shrugged when Tom tried to draw him out on this point. "The pin sounds like a more recent Hindu object—but I may be wrong."

"If the pin isn't valuable, why would those dacoits take so much trouble to steal it?"

"Perhaps because Kali is sacred to Indian thugs and dacoits," Mortlake replied.

Tom went back to his room. He was convinced that Mortlake's surprise had been genuine and that the man had been truthful about the pin being planted. Nevertheless, to play safe, Tom made a hasty trip to the *Sky Queen* and radioed Ames at Enterprises to check Mortlake's background.

Next morning Prince Jahan offered to escort

Tom, Bud, and the girls on a brief tour of Chullagar. As the young people left the palace, they saw the mahouts washing the royal elephants outside the stables. Chow was helping them!

"He must have taken a shine to that elephant he rode yesterday," Tom said with a chuckle.

The Texan was whistling happily as he sloshed water over the huge beast's wrinkled gray hide. "Hi, folks!" Chow called. "Figgered an ole Texas wrangler like me oughta get acquainted with the ridin' stock around here."

Sandy giggled. "The elephant certainly looks as if he's enjoying that bath. You two seem to be pretty good friends."

"Yup, we sorta understand each other. Only it's a she. Her name's Chini, meanin' 'Sugar.'" Chow added, "She's got false teeth."

"False teeth! Are you serious?" asked Phyl.

"Sure. Bein' a lady, her tusks don't grow very big, so they fit her up with wooden ones." Chow tugged at one white-painted tusk to show how it came loose. "Fer parades, they even gild her toenails. An' you know what? These critters are ticklish!"

"With those thick hides?" Bud scoffed.

"Honest Injun—I'll show you." Chow ran his fingers softly over the elephant's flank.

A mahout bringing a fresh bucket of water exclaimed, "Stop, Sahib—that is dangerous!"

The warning came too late! The elephant

reared skittishly and trumpeted. Then the beast plunged its trunk into the bucket of water and sprayed Chow from head to foot! Chow stood spluttering and dripping while his audience shook with laughter.

"Brand my poncho," Chow mumbled, "I shoulda knowed better'n to get fresh with a lady!"

A horse-drawn carriage took Prince Jahan's party through the city. The streets were noisy as mountaineers and peasants poured into Chullagar for the festival. Heavily loaded yaks plodded along, jostled by mule caravans which were driven by jolly fur-hatted Tibetans. The men wore turquoise and coral earrings, and their animals were decorated with red pompoms of yak hair.

Prayer flags were draped across the fronts of buildings, and many of the whitewashed brick houses were being repainted pink, yellow, or blue in honor of the Feast of Chogyal. As the carriage passed, there were shouts of *"Jai Kumar* Jahan!— Long live Prince Jahan!"

"They seem to like you." Phyl said to him.

The market place was a babble of voices. Street vendors spread their wares on the pavements. One turbaned, gray-bearded rug merchant sat puffing on a hubble-bubble pipe. A stall displayed clusters of rainbow-colored spun-glass bracelets. A dye seller was weighing heaps of powder on scales.

"You must watch out when the festival is in full swing," Jahan warned Sandy and Phyl. "The merrymakers brew colored water with those dyes and splash everyone in sight."

The girls noticed that many of the women wore ring ornaments looped through one nostril. Jahan said that these were comparable to the wedding rings worn by Western women. Here and there squatted yellow-robed Buddhist monks, holding out their required begging bowls.

Lamas, or temple priests, with drooping mustaches strolled along spinning small cylinders, called prayer wheels, mounted atop their staffs. The cylinders, Jahan explained, held written prayers which were believed to be wafted up to heaven by the spinning.

Tom was scanning the shop signs. Presently the carriage passed one which bore a name, both in English and in Hindi: CHULLAGAR TRADING COMPANY. Tom asked the driver to stop. After making a hasty excuse to Prince Jahan and the girls, he and Bud jumped out.

"This is the outfit that Mr. Mukerji said ships him goods from Vishnapur," the young inventor reminded his pal. "Someone at this end must be part of the spy plot."

To their surprise, the shop was locked. A woman, red-eyed from weeping, answered their knock. She told the boys her husband had been arrested the night before by Prince Gopal's security police. She did not know why.

Bud said to Tom, "Gopal must have hauled him in for questioning to find out how that Kali pin turned up in Bombay." Tom nodded thoughtfully.

That afternoon the Americans witnessed an archery contest and visited several temples and shrines. The next day Sandy and Phyl were invited to accompany the Rani to several public functions, so Tom proposed to Prince Jahan that he and his fellow trainees take a sightseeing flight with him and Bud over Vishnapur in the *Sky Queen*. Jahan was delighted.

The sleek silver craft took off from the airfield and headed northward. Tom and Bud were amazed at the gorgeous variety of the scenery. Rice-terraced slopes rose upward from valleys strewn with lush tropical forests. At higher levels, the slopes flattened into bleak plateaus, slashed by breath-taking gorges. Here and there could be seen a lonely hilltop monastery or a mud-walled mountain village.

In the distance ghostly, snow-capped peaks soared against the sky. Jahan pointed to the most majestic, murmuring, "That is Chogyal."

Presently they passed over a broad, treeless valley. In the midst of the valley floor lay a dark-green lake. A line of moving specks indicated a train of pack mules, but otherwise there was no sign of human life or habitation.

Tom was struck by the stark loneliness of the scene. "Boy, there's a grim-looking spot!"

"Grim indeed, my friend—that lake is poison-ous," said Jahan. "It is the Lake of Kali."

Kali! Tom and Bud exchanged startled glances.

"What makes the lake poisonous?" Bud asked.

Prince Jahan shrugged. "I do not know, but as

you see, no vegetation can exist near it. Were it not for the lake, this valley could be turned into rich farmland to feed many of our people."

Tom was curious to know more. He landed near the lake, then scooped up a sample of the murky water in a bottle. Using a Swift spectroscope and a gas chromatograph, he analyzed it aboard the Flying Lab. The test showed an organic substance containing chlorine, carbon, and nitrogen.

"So the poison must be due to some plant growth in the water, rather than minerals in the soil," he told Prince Jahan.

By now, the pack caravan with its tinkling bells was approaching the *Sky Queen*. The native mule drivers, awed by the huge plane, halted to chat with Tom's party.

One, whose remarks were translated by Gyong, told of seeing a weird monster enter and rise from the lake at night!

"Yes, yes, Sahibs," said another muleteer. "Many spirits about! Sometimes they make fountains of fire rise from the mountains!"

CHAPTER X

SKY SHOW

FOUNTAINS of fire! Once again Tom shot a startled glance at Bud. This sounded suspiciously like rocket launching!

Tom asked the mule driver, "You see this fire only at night?"

"Yes, Sahib." The bare-legged, wool-capped mountaineer nodded vigorously. "The fire shoots up high, high in the sky!"

"Sounds like a spaceship going up," Bud muttered.

"Right. This might be a clue to the base of the mysterious rocket ship!" Aloud he asked the driver, "Where do you see this fire?"

The man pointed to the north. "Near the flanks of Chogyal. Maybe the mountain god is lighting the sky for his festival—eh, Sahib?"

Rakshi had come over and broke in sneeringly,

"A fine story—fountains of fire in the sky and a monster in the lake! Now you can see what we shall have to contend with if we ever hope to educate these ignorant fools."

"Folk stories often have some truth in them," Tom said. "Even in Scotland, they talk about a monster being seen in Loch Ness." Turning to Gyong, the young inventor added, "Please ask the other man to tell us more about this lake monster."

Gyong did so and then translated the reply. "He says it is huge—big enough to devour a man. Its coat is scaly and it has two round glittering eyes. Sometimes it walks on its hind legs and sometimes crawls on all fours."

Prince Jahan looked at Tom quizzically. "You seem very much interested in the Lake of Kali. Since you took the trouble to analyze the poison, perhaps you have something in mind?"

"Not exactly," Tom answered. "Tell me—does this lake ever overflow its banks in the rainy season?"

The mule drivers and the student engineers agreed that this never happened.

"In that case, the lake probably isn't spring-fed," Tom deduced. "More likely it's connected with an underground river system in such a way that hydrostatic pressure keeps the lake from ever rising above its normal level. Jahan, would you allow me to bring over a geologist to make soundings? There might be a way to purify this lake."

Jahan's eyes shone. "Of course! If this region could be made livable, I could turn the valley into a model farmland!"

"Whoa! Slow down!" Tom smiled. "I have a wild idea, that's all. It may not work out, so let's not even talk about it yet."

As they flew back to Chullagar, Tom radioed Enterprises. He told his father about the strange poison lake and asked that an expert be sent over at once to make Geophone soundings.

"I think I know just the man for the job, son. I'll get in touch with him right away," Mr. Swift promised. "Incidentally, Harlan Ames has a report for you on Hugh Mortlake. Hold on."

Ames's voice came over the receiver. "Mortlake's story checks out, skipper. The Vroom Museum says he has worked on their staff for ten years and is one of the country's leading authorities on Indian and Oriental art."

Tom thanked Ames and signed off. During the rest of the flight he puzzled silently over the mystery. Who had put the Kali pin in Mortlake's luggage and why? Tom had no clues.

In a short while the young inventor prepared to land at the Chullagar airfield. On their way to the palace, he and Bud noticed that the town was decked with flowers and painted effigies of gods and demons.

"Tomorrow is Chogyal's main feast day," Jahan explained. "There will be a great procession and at night a dazzling display of fireworks."

Tom said nothing to the others, but later he returned to the *Sky Queen* and made another radio call to Enterprises. His face wore a big grin as he planned for an addition to the evening's entertainment.

That evening Tom sat next to Prince Gopal at dinner. "I hear you wish to bring a geologist from America," Gopal said politely, "to locate the water source of the Lake of Kali."

"Yes. Prince Jahan has given his permission."

"And when you have found the source, what then? You have plans to purify the lake?"

Tom shrugged. "There might be a way to bring in fresh water. But I really can't tell yet."

"Most interesting," Gopal murmured. "But I must warn you that many of our people are fearful and superstitious. The Lake of Kali is already an object of dread. To tamper with it might provoke serious trouble."

"I'm not sure I understand." Tom frowned.

Gopal said, "There is great unrest. The Rajah cannot afford to displease the people."

Tom stared in surprise at the dewan. "You mean there might be a revolution? But Prince Jahan seems very popular with his subjects."

"Appearances are deceiving. There are always hotheads eager to stir up trouble."

"I see." Tom nodded thoughtfully. "I'll remember what you've told me, sir."

The great Festival of Chogyal began the next morning with the grand final archery tournament. The Rajah, with his court and guests, watched from under silk canopies.

First the archers paraded onto the field, bearing gay-colored flags on poles and wearing knee-length kimonos. Each man bowed low before the Rajah and Rani. The archers were followed by priests who blessed the field, bows, arrows, and targets. Then heralds blew blasts on six-foot trumpets and the contest began.

Each team had its own witch doctor and troupe of bejeweled dancing girls. Part of the girls' job was to sing the praises of their own archers and insult the opposing team. The contestants shot at the targets with bamboo bows and copper-tipped arrows.

"This is like a mixture of Robin Hood and the Arabian Nights!" Sandy exclaimed to Bud.

During an intermission, yellow-skirted male dancers with feathered crowns whirled about the field to the music of drums, trumpets, and bells. When the contest was over, the Rajah presented a bag of gold pieces to the winning team.

"That was an amazing performance," Tom said, and Bud added, "I'd hate to be in the path of one of those arrows!"

After a palace lunch of pork, bamboo shoots,

and saffron rice, the teen-agers hurried to a fairground outside town. It was dotted with yakskin tents put up by peasants who had journeyed over mountain trails to the festival.

Trinket sellers, jugglers, and snake charmers plied their trade among the crowds. There was even a small, crude wooden Ferris wheel which two men were turning by hand. Sandy, Phyl, Tom, and Bud took a ride and the two girls squealed with delight as they clung to the swinglike open seats.

"This is even more fun than the big ones back home!" Phyl exclaimed breathlessly.

At two o'clock the foursome returned to Chullagar for the great parade. The town seemed to explode with color and noise as the procession wound its way through the streets.

First came yellow-hatted Hindu priests chanting hymns—musicians blowing oboes—and temple lamas, in queer red hats with ear flaps, spinning prayer wheels. These were followed by masked demon dancers who pranced to the sound of drums and gongs.

Then came several loud military bands and troops of soldiers. Among them were turbaned Indians, bagpipers, Gurkhas from Nepal, and the Rajah's red-coated Royal Guard armed with muzzle-loaders.

Suddenly an outburst of cheers and yells went up as the royal elephants came into view.

Tom was goggle-eyed. "Am I seeing things," he shouted to Bud above the din, "or is that Chow Winkler riding the lead elephant?"

"It's the Texas Kid himself!" Bud yelled back.

Chow—resplendent in a ten-gallon hat, fancy breeches, and red-orange cowboy shirt—was perched on his favorite elephant's neck. He was spinning a lariat and doing rope tricks that brought shrieks of approval from the crowd.

Chini the elephant was wearing gold caps on her tusks, silver anklets, and brocaded trappings. Her trunk was painted with flowers.

Chow doffed his hat with one hand as he sighted Tom's party. "Hi there, ladies an' buckaroos! How'm I doin'?"

"Terrific!" Sandy called back.

More elephants followed, bearing Prince Jahan, Prince Gopal, and finally the Rajah and Rani.

Musicians blaring singsong tunes, capering masked gods, and demons brought up the rear. The parade was scarcely over before the crowds broke into wild street dancing. Colored water was sprayed in all directions, and both Tom and Bud were liberally streaked with dye.

"Too bad Swift Enterprises couldn't have had a float in the parade!" Phyl remarked with a giggle as they walked back to the palace.

"Don't count us out too soon," Tom replied mysteriously. Bud and the girls peppered him with questions, but he refused to say more.

Toward the end of the afternoon a Swift cargo jet touched down on the Chullagar airfield. Tom received word of its arrival and hurried to the airfield to meet it. Aboard was a young geologist named Bill Harper.

Soon after dark the royal court gathered outside the palace for the fireworks display. Rockets streaked across the sky and burst into glowing fireballs or scattered stars and meteors in every color of the rainbow. Huge set pieces turned into flaming dragons, demons, and monsters.

"What's keeping Tom?" Phyl asked her companions.

"Search me," said Bud, glancing around. "He said he'd be out here."

Suddenly Tom's voice blared from a number of loud-speakers:

"This is one of Prince Jahan's friends from America, bringing greetings to the people of Vishnapur! Through the magic of science, you will now see scenes from the country where your prince has been visiting."

Other voices followed, translating Tom's words into Hindi and Tibetan dialects. Then a huge likeness of the capitol dome in Washington sprang into view in the night sky.

"Tom's using his three-D telejector!" Bud gasped. This amazing invention could project three-dimensional images of any size, without a screen and in full color.

Views of skyscrapered cities, broad expressways, farms, factories, and schools appeared in the sky, one after another. Tom and his translators kept up a stream of comments.

When the sky show was over, there was an awed hush—then a loud outburst of shouts and cheers. The Rajah summoned Tom and thanked him personally.

When Tom rejoined Bud and the girls, Sandy burst out, "The show was great. But how did you ever manage to put it on at such short notice?"

"Nothing to it, Sis." Tom grinned. "After Jahan told me about the parade and fireworks, I radioed Enterprises to send my telejector pronto. The travelogue was taped two months ago for the U. S. Information Agency."

Late that night the two boys returned to their room in the palace. Tom opened the door and switched on the light, then gasped.

"Good grief!" Bud said in a hoarse whisper.

A blood-chilling, four-armed figure of the goddess Kali had been painted in red on the wall near their beds. Below were the words:

Do Not Touch My Lake Or You Will Die!

CHAPTER XI

FLIGHT INTO DANGER

TOGETHER, Tom and Bud walked over to examine the strange warning. The death goddess's teeth appeared to be dripping blood, and a ring of skulls had been painted around her neck.

"Whew! What a cheerful thing to see just before hitting the sack!" Bud muttered.

Tom's jaw set grimly. "We'd better tell Prince Gopal about this."

Tom found a servant, who hurried to notify the dewan. Prince Gopal came to the boys' room. A look of alarm spread over his face when he saw the sinister painting.

"When did this happen?" he asked.

Tom replied, "It wasn't here when we came back to our room after dinner."

"No doubt it was done during the fireworks display," Gopal said. "Many of the guards and servants left their posts to watch the sky spectacle.

The culprit may have slipped in through a window."

"Looks to me like the work of more dacoits," Bud put in. "Maybe the same gang who stole Sandy's Kali pin and attacked Prince Jahan."

"You may be right," Gopal agreed. "I fear this may be only the first hint of worse trouble to come."

Tom said, "You take the warning seriously?"

"Most seriously!" Gopal snapped. "I have told you that tampering with the Lake of Kali may provoke an outbreak among the people. Now it appears that your own life is in danger."

The dewan strode back and forth, twisting his mustache. Then he faced Tom. "I trust you will now reconsider your foolhardy plans."

"As I told you last night, sir, I've made no plans yet," the young inventor replied coolly. "What happens after I get more data on the lake will be up to Prince Jahan and the Rajah."

Gopal's dark eyes gleamed with anger, but when he spoke, his voice was cold and polite. "Very well. But you now know the risk you are taking. Good night, gentlemen."

The dewan strode out of the room. Soon a servant appeared to clean the gruesome painting off the wall. He was nervous and fearful.

As the boys got ready for bed, Bud chuckled. "Knowing what a stubborn clunk you are, I suppose a mere death threat won't stop you."

"Bud, the peasants in this country don't look exactly overfed," Tom replied. "If purifying that lake will make new farmland for these people, I'm going right ahead in spite of Kali and her stooges."

Next morning Tom reported the incident to Jahan. The prince frowned when he heard about the threat. He was silent for a moment, then said, "That valley could feed many mouths if it were irrigated with good water. I am not afraid of a few fanatics—but there is your own safety to think of, Tom."

"If you're willing to go ahead, so am I."

"Then it is settled."

Tom told Bill Harper, the geologist, that they would take off in the *Sky Queen* at ten o'clock. A little later Hugh Mortlake accosted Tom in a corridor of the palace.

"I hear you're flying north," the archaeologist said. "Could you take me to Shankaru?"

"I guess so—if you have permission."

"That's all set," Mortlake assured him.

The other trainees were eager to accompany Prince Jahan and the young scientist. As the group was boarding the Flying Lab, Hugh Mortlake came hurrying across the airfield with two palace servants lugging his baggage.

"You are coming with us?" Rakshi inquired.

"Tom Swift has kindly promised to drop me at Shankaru," Mortlake explained.

"Shankaru?" Rakshi's eyes blazed. *"Nahin,* my friend—you are mistaken! That site is closed to pilfering foreign treasure hunters!"

"Chup raho!—Be silent!"

Rakshi turned and found himself confronting Jahan, whose face was flushed with anger.

"Mr. Mortlake has my permission to investigate the ruins at Shankaru," Jahan said icily. "Apologize to him at once—and never again speak with such discourtesy to a royal guest!"

Rakshi obeyed sullenly.

Tom and his crew warmed up the atomic jet and the huge plane soon took off. After a short flight from Chullagar, the ship settled down over the desolate gray-brown valley near the Lake of Kali. While Bill Harper was unloading his equipment, Tom remarked to Prince Jahan:

"It'll take Bill a while to plant his receivers and make his soundings. Want to come along while I fly Mr. Mortlake to Shankaru? After that, I'd like to cruise over the mountains and try to spot the river that feeds this lake."

Jahan was thrilled at the chance to view the mighty Himalayan ramparts from the air. "Parts of the range around Chogyal have never been mapped," he told Tom. "The exact frontier is disputed by our northern neighbor."

It was arranged that the other student engineers and Bud would remain at the lake to help Bill. Before the *Queen* took off, Bud drew Tom aside.

"Something tells me you're going to scout for more than a river," he said.

Tom nodded. "Maybe a rocket-ship base, too."

"Good luck, pal. And watch your step!"

Skimming over the rugged crags and valleys, Tom soon landed Mortlake at Shankaru. The only remains at the ancient site were crumbling walls and columns. Aside from a few distant herdsmen's huts, the spot seemed deserted.

"Sure you'll be all right here?" Tom asked.

"Quite sure, thank you," Mortlake replied as they shook hands in farewell. "I have a tent and enough supplies for several weeks."

"Caravans often pass by," Prince Jahan added.

"Well, I'm leaving you a two-way radio," Tom told the archaeologist, "so if you get in trouble, you can always contact Chullagar."

Again the Flying Lab took off. Shankaru lay in northeastern Vishnapur, while the Lake of Kali was in the northwest. Tom decided to cruise back along a curving arc that would carry them over the heart of the soaring Chogyal range.

Tom was filled with awe at the mountain scenery. The giant peaks, glistening white with snow and ice, seemed to stretch out endlessly before them in stark majesty.

"What a sight!" Tom murmured.

"Now you can see why many of my people worship the spirits of these mountains," Jahan replied.

Tom nodded and dipped through cloud layers to probe the gorges, valleys, and ridges. From time to time he spotted a lonely mountaineers' camp or village. Otherwise, there was no sign of life.

Suddenly a whistling roar split the air! Tom jerked his head around. A glowing exhaust trail was streaking across the sky, disappearing far behind them toward the left.

"A missile!" Tom gasped. He gunned the elevator jets and the *Queen* zoomed upward.

Jahan's eyes widened in fear. "Here comes another!" he cried, pointing to four o'clock.

Tom banked into a shrieking turn.

Bo-o-o-oom! A dazzling burst of fiery light filled the sky. The missile had crossed their hot exhaust trail and exploded! The *Sky Queen* shuddered, then steadied again on course.

Neither Tom nor Jahan spoke as the young inventor poured on speed. Moments later, the prince murmured in relief, "A narrow squeak! . . . We must have intruded over the airspace of our neighbor to the north!"

Inwardly Tom was jubilant as he glanced at his flight charts. They were well south of the disputed border area. He felt sure they had drawn the missile fire for a different reason. The *Sky Queen* must have passed close to the enemy secret rocket-ship base!

As they flew on, Tom scanned the terrain closely. The peaks and ridges became gentler.

The missile crossed their exhaust trail and exploded!

Presently Tom's eye caught the silver glint of flowing water. He swooped down and studied the scene through electronic binoculars.

"Ten to one we've found the water source for the Lake of Kali!"

He could see a cataract, fed by the mountain snows. It was pouring down a steep slope, only to disappear into a rocky cleft below. Tom suspected its underground flow must carry it somewhere beneath the lake. He pressed a button and an automatic aerial camera began clicking photographs.

Minutes later, the *Queen* landed near the poison lake. Bill Harper had just finished reading the Geophone tapes.

"Your hunch was right, Tom," he reported. "The water wells up through a single opening near the center of the lake basin. It's fed by an underground river channeling through the bedrock. The river must rise to lake level in the hills south of here. That's what keeps this basin from overflowing."

Tom's eyes kindled with excitement. "Then I'm sure the lake can be purified!"

"How?" asked Prince Jahan.

"By vaporizing the poisonous water with a giant burning lens attached to a spaceship!"

CHAPTER XII

TIGER HUNT

TOM'S listeners stared in amazement.

"A giant burning lens in the sky?" Jahan echoed. "Surely such a thing is impossible!"

"I don't mean a glass lens," the young inventor said with a smile. "This one would work on electromagnetic principles."

Before Tom could explain, a crewman came hurrying from the *Sky Queen*. He was holding a large, freshly developed photograph.

"Skipper, look at this!"

Tom turned. "Oh, hi, Vic! Got those prints all ready?"

"Not quite—but here's something odd."

Tom took the glossy photograph. A baffled frown spread over his face. The picture had been taken with a special Swift aerial camera equipped with a telephoto device that gave tremendous magnification. It was an enlargement showing part of the mountain slope near the cataract. In the drifted snow strange tracks could be seen!

"Good night!" Tom muttered. "Who or what leaves tracks like these?"

"That's what I'd like to know," Vic replied.

"Let's see," Bud said eagerly, peering over Tom's shoulder. Then he whistled. "Roarin' rockets! Is it beast, bird, or fish?"

The marks in the snow were somewhat like the footprints of an ape. But the toes were long and clawlike and seemed to be webbed.

"They look huge," Bud went on. "How big would they be, Vic?"

"Hard to tell," the crewman answered. "Going by the amount of magnification, I'd guess twice as big as a man's footprint."

Jahan and the others peered at the photograph. A strange look came over their faces.

"Yeti tracks!" Gyong murmured.

"What's that?" Tom asked.

"A yeti is what you in America would call an Abominable Snowman," Prince Jahan explained.

Tom and Bud exchanged startled glances. Both had often read reports of weird, apelike creatures said to inhabit the high Himalayas. Another thought occurred to Tom. Could these be the tracks of the lake monster?

"Bud, let's take the Skeeter and see if we can follow these prints!" he proposed.

"Great! I've always wanted to meet an Abominable Snowman!" Bud gulped comically.

The Skeeter, a tiny helicopter, was carried in a hangar compartment aboard the Flying Lab. The two boys wheeled out the craft and took off, heading toward the mountain cataract.

When they reached the area, Tom skimmed low until they picked up the tracks, then followed them downward. The trail was easy to see at first, but as they approached the timber line and the snow thinned out, the strange tracks could no longer be sighted. Tom explained his idea that the creature might be the lake monster reported by local natives.

"This bears out their stories," Bud agreed.

The Skeeter returned to the lake and the boys told of the results of their flight. Then Bill Harper reported that he had studied the other photographs of the mountain cataract. He, too, felt sure this was the source of the lake.

"You still have not told us, Tom," Jahan said eagerly, "what you meant by a giant burning lens that works on electromagnetic principles."

"Remember the electrostatic-field device that I demonstrated?" Tom replied. "I told you the field can be shaped to serve as a reflector for electromagnetic radiation. Well, by lofting my device into the sun—and by shaping the field with just the right amount of curvature—I'm sure I can beam down enough infrared radiation to vaporize the whole lake."

"But, Swift Sahib, the lake is large," said a student named Tundup. "To evaporate so much water would take vast amounts of energy."

Tom began to jot down some quick calculations. "Let's take five hundred watts per square centimeter as the power density I will focus on the lake surface. Now then, assuming the volume of water in the lake to be . . ."

In a few moments Tom had the answer. "By a conservative estimate, I should be able to boil away all the water in about six hours."

"Marvelous," said Prince Jahan.

With a malicious smile Rakshi put in, "But will not more water be welling up all the time from the underground river?"

"Not if I plug the inlet first," Tom replied quietly. "After the water has been vaporized, I can clean out all the poisonous sediment and plant growth with a machine of mine called a spectro-marine selector. Then I'll remove the plug and allow the lake basin to fill up again—with pure, fresh water."

The young Asian engineers burst into loud applause for Tom Swift's amazing scheme.

"Are you willing to undertake the project?" Jahan asked Tom.

Tom ran his fingers thoughtfully through his blond crew cut. "Yes—but it would have to take second place to the Mars rocket job. And what about getting your father's approval?"

"We shall ask him tonight," said Jahan.

On the flight back to Chullagar, Tom radioed home to his father to check on the progress of his rocket retriever and the spacecraft to carry it. Mr. Swift told him the vehicle was nearing completion and would be ready for a test flight on the following Monday.

When Tom described his plan for purifying the Lake of Kali, the elder scientist readily approved the project. "If your plan works, it could win a lot of friends for America in that part of the world," Mr. Swift pointed out. "By the way, have you caught any American news broadcasts in the past twelve hours?"

"No, Dad. Why?"

"An American research satellite, the *Ionos II,* has disappeared from the sky."

"Disappeared?" Tom echoed. "How?"

"No one knows," Mr. Swift replied. "Our tracking stations all over the world have been hunting for it with radar, but apparently it's just not up there. Of course, it might have been knocked out of orbit by a meteorite and burned up in the atmosphere."

"The odds against a direct hit strong enough to do that would be pretty great," Tom said, and his father agreed.

The youth signed off with a puzzled frown.

That evening the young inventor was granted a special audience with Rajah Krishna. Prince Jahan and Prince Gopal were also on hand to hear Tom explain his amazing scheme.

The Rajah listened intently and seemed to be much impressed. His hawklike gaze never left the young inventor's face while Tom was speaking.

"Truly, this is a bold plan, Shri Swift." The Rajah frowned thoughtfully and stroked his beard. "But might not the vapor from the boiling lake spread poison over the land?"

Tom shook his head. "No, your highness. The vapor would rise, dissipate quickly into the upper atmosphere, and leave the poison in the lake bed."

"Hmm. If the valley could be turned into farmland, it would be a great boon to our ill-fed mountain people." The Rajah turned to his dewan. "What is your opinion, Gopal?"

"I, too, admire Shri Swift's scientific boldness, your highness. But our people are superstitious and fear Kali's power. I am not sure—"

He broke off as a commotion sounded outside the palace. Prince Jahan strode to a jalousied door leading out onto a balcony. Tom and the others followed. As they stepped outside, Tom could see a ragged-looking crowd gathered below. They were shouting wildly and waving their arms. Tom could understand nothing of what they were saying except for the frenzied chant:

"Kali! . . . Kali! . . . Kali!"

Gopal urged the Rajah, Jahan, and Tom to go back inside. Then he shouted something to the palace guards. There were sounds of a tussle below, but quiet was finally restored.

"What's wrong?" Tom asked Jahan.

"The news of your plan has leaked out. The mob was shouting that Kali would be angered if her lake is drained."

Gopal's face was grim as he came in from the balcony. "Your highness, it may not be wise for Shri Swift to proceed with his project."

Jahan protested that a small, superstitious mob should not be allowed to block Vishnapur's progress. But the Rajah silenced him sternly with a wave of his jeweled hand.

"Shri Swift's plan is good. But Gopal's advice must also be weighed seriously. I shall decide later."

Tom was keenly disappointed. But he could see that Jahan did not dare oppose his father's decision.

Rajah Krishna turned to the young inventor with a polite smile. "Please do not think your plan is not appreciated. As a climax to your visit, I have ordered a *shikar,* or hunt, to be held tomorrow in your honor. A tiger has been sighted by villagers near here."

Tom was embarrassed. Neither he nor Tom Sr. cared to hunt wild animals, but he did not like to refuse the Rajah's invitation. Tactfully he explained that he preferred a camera to a gun. Rajah Krishna promised that arrangements would be made for Tom to photograph the hunt.

Sandy and Phyl were included in the invitation. But when Tom told them what it was, the girls expressed distaste. "The Rani's giving a tea tomorrow," Sandy said, "so that excuses us."

Next morning the royal hunting party set out on elephants for a lowland village near Chullagar. The headman of the village reported that the tiger had killed two cows and a bull in the past few days. Fresh pug marks of the huge cat could be seen entering a patch of jungle at one end of a small, narrow valley.

Prince Gopal, a crack big-game hunter, took charge of the hunt. He ordered men from the village, beating sticks and pans—along with native *shikaris,* or huntsmen, riding elephants—to enter the woods and drive the tiger out through the valley. The Rajah, Prince Jahan, and Gopal himself would sit in *machans*—tree platforms built at the far end of the valley. They would carry rifles, and be ready to shoot the beast as it tried to escape.

"What about Tom and me?" Bud asked.

Prince Gopal said the boys would be posted on an elephant, well forward of the machans, so they would have ample time to photograph the tiger before it was killed. Chow, who had come along on Chini, wanted the boys to sit with him on his mount. But Gopal said a more experienced mahout should handle this job.

As the hunt got under way, Tom and Bud's elephant lumbered into position. The boys sat in a boxlike hunting howdah roped to the elephant's back.

"This howdah sure seems loose," Bud grumbled as the conveyance jiggled back and forth.

The two boys checked their movie cameras. Tom turned for a moment to stare through binoculars at the machans several hundred yards behind.

The boys' mount was standing in thick undergrowth. Presently Tom and Bud could hear the *thunk-thunk-thunk* of the beaters advancing through the jungled valley. The boys' hearts pounded faster.

"There's the tiger!" Bud yelled.

Their cameras began to whir as the swift-moving orange-and-black beast burst from cover some distance ahead.

Suddenly their elephant trumpeted in pain and reared up wildly on its hind feet. The two boys were hurled from their howdah. They lay directly in the path of the oncoming tiger!

CHAPTER XIII

DEADLY QUILLS

THOUGH dazed, Tom scrambled to his feet. Bud was lying nearby, stunned. The boys' elephant, heedless of the mahout's sharp goad, was lumbering off toward the hillside, the howdah tilting at a crazy angle.

Tom's throat went dry. The huge tiger was advancing with quick, powerful strides, its emerald-green eyes fixed balefully on the young inventor.

There was no time to drag Bud to safety. Tom tried to think coolly. Suddenly he remembered hearing that tigers would seldom attack humans unless hunger drove them to become man-eaters.

The beast gave a blood-chilling growl. Tom, standing over Bud, waved and shouted at it. The beast veered aside.

The next second, the huge cat leaped into the

air. Then Tom saw a long, thin quill sticking in its jowl! The annoyed tiger writhed and came down on all fours, snarling in pain and rage. With a roar it charged at the two boys!

Just then Tom heard a wild whoop and saw another elephant lumbering down the opposite hillside. Chow astride Chini! The tiger halted, gave a quick glance, and fled off down the valley.

By this time the Rajah, Jahan, and Gopal had climbed down from their tree platforms and were also running to Tom's aid. Too late the tiger, realized it was heading into fresh danger. Jahan's rifle cracked, then Gopal's, and the mighty beast dropped.

Tom was soaked with cold perspiration. He was ready to hug Chow as the loyal cowpoke swung down from his mount.

"Brand my six-guns, I knowed you two shoulda ridden Chini!" Chow gabbled. "You okay, boss?"

"S-s-sure, I'm all right. Help me with Bud."

Jahan, the Rajah, and Prince Gopal came hurrying through the jungle growth to join them. Bud soon revived, having suffered nothing worse than a bump on the head. He smiled his thanks upon hearing he had been saved from the tiger's attack.

By this time the beaters were emerging from the woods. Tom and Bud's mahout also returned, shamefaced and on foot, leading his elephant. Prince Gopal turned on him, furious.

The mahout cringed. "Please, Sahib—I could not help it! It was *kantedukkar* that made the elephant act so! I pulled this from his trunk." He held out a long, thin quill.

"What's *kantedukkar?*" Bud asked.

"A porcupine," Prince Jahan translated. "The tiger must have encountered one also."

"I reckon that would drive an elephant loco," Chow said. "Their trunks is real tender."

"All this does not excuse what happened to the howdah!" Prince Gopal said. Then he angrily questioned the mahout as Jahan translated. "Why were the girth ropes not tightly secured, you fool?"

The cowering elephant driver wrung his hands. "I do not know, Sahib! They were tight when we left Chullagar. I fastened them myself."

"Then it is you who shall pay for allowing them to come loose!" Gopal retorted. "You shall be beaten!"

Tom interceded, asking that the man not be punished and Prince Gopal reluctantly agreed. The mahout knelt gratefully to Tom.

"Shri Swift," said the Rajah, "you are a brave young man."

"I was scared out of my wits, your highness," Tom replied bluntly.

"Yet you stood by your friend and faced a charging tiger. This American mahout Chow also showed great courage in riding to your rescue."

Chow squirmed at the praise. "Shucks, I was safe on this good ole elephant," he mumbled.

Rajah Krishna went on, "In reward for such bravery by both of you, Shri Swift, I have decided that you may proceed with your plan to drain the Lake of Kali."

Tom's eyes flashed with excitement. "Thank you, your highness!" he exclaimed, and Jahan wrung his hand warmly. Bud clapped him on the back.

While the dead tiger was being loaded onto an elephant, Tom strolled about among the jungle growth. He appeared to be admiring the wild orchids and listening to the chatter of the langur monkeys. But Bud noticed that he seemed silent and absorbed as the shikar headed back to the village.

"A rupee for your thoughts, pal," Bud muttered. "You weren't really looking at the posies, were you?"

Tom shook his head. "No, I was searching for a spot where someone might have been hiding."

"Hiding?" Bud narrowed his eyes. "How come?"

"Those porcupine quills were stiff and straight," Tom said. "They could have been fired from a blowgun to make our elephant bolt and enrage the tiger."

"Wow! You mean someone tried to kill us?"

"It's possible. And the same person could have loosened the girth ropes on the howdah."

Bud gave a low whistle. "But who?"

"Good question. If we knew the answer, we might also know who plotted the spy setup."

That evening a feast was held at the palace to celebrate the shikar and end the festival. Sunday, after good-byes and a promise to return soon,

Tom's group and the trainees took off for the United States.

At his homecoming dinner in Shopton that same day, Mr. Swift informed Tom that his rocket retriever craft was ready and had been moved to Fearing Island for its test flight. He added, "The newspaper and TV people are clamoring for a look at it, so we've arranged a press showing at the base tomorrow afternoon."

"Let's hope no bugs develop!" Tom said, grinning.

Early Monday morning he flew to Fearing with Bud, eager to see his creation. Viewed from the side, the new spaceship looked like a fat, tilted crescent moon—its horns pointing up and back. The lower horn extended far aft to form the tail of the craft, with a huge crystal sphere mounted at the stern. Atop the upper horn was a bubble observation dome, while the pilot's window looked out from the forward bulge of the crescent.

"She's a beauty, Tom!" Bud commented. He pointed to several dish-shaped antennas mounted on the ship's "spine" along the inner curve of the crescent. "These are the repelatron catchers?"

"That's right. And the rocket—or whatever other space object is retrieved—will be held right here, inside the curve of the fuselage, with magnetic grapples to keep it in place."

"Got a name for her yet?"

Tom smiled. "Well, as you know, that double-walled crystal sphere at the stern is my electro-static-field device. I've decided to call the gadget a 'dynasphere'—or 'polar-ray dynasphere,' thanks to you, pal. Remember you used the term 'polar-ray beam' when I was demonstrating this device?"

The two boys entered the craft's flight compartment. Tom gave Bud a check-out on the controls, which were like the *Challenger's* but simpler. Then they climbed a steel ladder to the observation dome.

"The dynasphere and the repelatron catchers will be operated from this board," Tom said as he showed Bud an electronic console. "The duplicate panel down in the flight compartment will be for emergencies."

"Sounds great! Let's take her up!"

Hurrying below to the main deck, the boys took their places at the controls. Tom called Base Communications for clearance, then switched on power. Lights flashed on the element-selector panel and a low hum filled the cabin as he tuned the ship's main-drive repelatrons for ground thrust.

Meanwhile, word had spread like wildfire that the strange new craft was about to be test-flown. Crewmen came swarming out of workshops and hangars to watch the take-off. A chorus of cheers arose as the ship zoomed aloft.

Soaring above the atmosphere, the two young astronauts circled oceans and continents in a three-hour orbit.

Bud was enthusiastic. "It's a real dream ship, skipper! . . . Did you say you're going to turn it over to the government after you retrieve the Mars rocket?"

"Yes, Bud. It'll be used for salvaging dead satellites and other space junk."

"Too bad we can't keep it," Bud said regretfully. Then he chuckled. "Say, I have just the name for this crate—Flying Junkwagon!"

Tom was still laughing as they landed. The boys climbed out of the spaceship and were greeted by a crowd of engineers and technicians eager for a report. Among them was Mr. Swift.

"A-OK—all the way!" Tom said.

"That's great news, son!"

During the afternoon, the young inventor posed for newsreel and television cameras and answered a barrage of questions from reporters. On Tom's orders Prince Jahan and the other Vishnapurian trainees were brought to the island in the *Sky Queen* and given a look at the Flying Junkwagon. Afterward, Tom and Bud had dinner with the group in the lounge of the Flying Lab.

"Tomorrow Bud and I are going up again to test the dynasphere," Tom announced. "We'll try to retrieve a dead American weather satellite—

sort of a dummy run for the Mars rocket job. Would you fellows like to observe?"

Jahan and his countrymen eagerly accepted.

"Then bunk aboard the *Queen* tonight," Tom told them. "One request, though—please consider the lab section as off limits. I'll be working in there. Hank Sterling sent along some blueprints of the dynasphere that I want to check over tonight."

Later, Tom excused himself and went to the plane's laboratory. It was nearly midnight when he emerged. His guests had retired, but just to make sure, Tom checked in the bunk room. He left and set out for the rocket-base sleeping quarters which he shared with Bud.

"If one of those Vishnapurians tries anything funny tonight, I'll use my special gadget to spot him," the young inventor thought as he slipped under the covers.

CHAPTER XIV

THE KIDNAPPED SATELLITE

THE following morning Tom and Bud returned to the *Sky Queen* to have breakfast with the trainee group. While they were still at the table, Tom excused himself.

He rejoined them in a little while, bringing a small, dark-glassed bulb with a reflector and electric cord. He plugged it into a socket and then asked Chow to close the window curtains and switch off the lights.

"Are you going to show us an experiment, Tom?" Prince Jahan asked with keen interest.

"Yes—sort of a fortune-telling experiment."

The young inventor asked everyone to put their hands on the table. Then he flicked on the portable black light. The guests exclaimed in surprise. *One pair of hands on the table shone with a greenish glow!*

"Whose hands are those?" asked Tundup.

"Rakshi's," said Gyong. "What does it mean?"

Tom told Chow to turn on the lights again and then replied, "I'm afraid it means Rakshi's 'fortune' doesn't look bright. You see, he's a spy and a thief—and probably the person who tried to incriminate Prince Jahan."

Rakshi sprang to his feet, pale and quivering. "How dare you accuse me of such things?"

"Save your breath," Tom said coldly. "That luminous dye on your hands came from the blueprints of the dynasphere in the *Queen's* lab. The prints are phonies. I just used them as bait."

Rakshi broke into loud ranting, but Prince Jahan silenced him curtly.

Tom went on, "Rakshi, if you're innocent, you won't mind being searched. No doubt you brought along a minature camera to snap whatever pictures you could at the base. When you sneaked in to look at the blueprints, you probably photographed those, too."

Bud moved toward Rakshi. But the young Asian whipped out a thin, curved dagger. His eyes glittering, he hissed, "I shall kill anyone who gets in my way!"

Rakshi darted toward the door. Chow would have tried to block his escape, but Tom shouted, "Don't, Chow! Let him go!"

The Texan fumed. "Boss, you're not goin' to let that sidewinder escape, are you?"

"I think he'll find it pretty hard to escape."

Tom strode to the windows and pulled aside the curtains. The others joined him. By this time, Rakshi was dashing across the airfield. Two small craft stood on the field—a helicopter and a sleek little Swift plane called a Pigeon Special. Rakshi headed for the copter, leaped aboard, and gunned the rotors.

Tom pulled out his pocket pencil radio and called the tower. Then he said to the others, "Come on outside and we'll see what happens."

As the group climbed down from the *Queen's* boarding ladder and peered up at the sky, they could see Rakshi's helicopter whirring aloft. Several small drone planes were circling in the blue. One darted from formation and dived at the helicopter with a whistling shriek.

"He's nailed!" Bud cried a moment later.

The interceptor drone banked sharply and began gliding down toward the airfield. The helicopter followed helplessly.

"How was it done, Tom?" Jahan asked.

"By an invention of mine called a landing forcer," Tom explained quietly. "The gadget's controlled from the tower."

Several security guards dashed out on the field as the helicopter touched down. Rakshi put up a violent struggle but was soon overpowered and handcuffed. Tom and Ames went to Base Security with Jahan to question the prisoner.

As Tom had suspected, Rakshi was found to be

carrying a miniature camera. But no amount of grilling could shake his sneering silence.

Ames said in disgust, "Keep him under tight guard and turn him over to the proper authorities."

As Jahan and Tom left the Security Office, the prince asked, "What will happen to Rakshi?"

"We have enough evidence to send him to prison for espionage. But in some cases, spies are deported. Perhaps the U. S. State Department will do that."

"My father would certainly prefer that. Rakshi is one of our people. He has brought shame to us, and it is our responsibility to see that he pays for his crime. Rest assured he will be punished severely in Vishnapur."

"I think the State Department will understand and cooperate. After all, our governments are on friendly terms," Tom assured him. "But remember the real brains behind this plot is probably still at large in your own country. Susak died without talking."

"No doubt my uncle, Prince Gopal, will know how to make Rakshi talk."

Soon afterward, Mr. and Mrs. Swift arrived on the island with Sandy and Phyl to watch the boys take off on their satellite recovery test.

"Sandy wants to christen the new spaceship, Tom," said Mr. Swift. "She and Phyl have a name all picked out. Okay with you?"

"Sure." Tom chuckled. "It's bound to be better than Flying Junkwagon!"

They drove to the launching area and Sandy unwrapped a bottle of ginger ale. The others accompanied her as she walked up to the craft. With a neat swing Sandy cracked the bottle across the fuselage, saying:

"I christen thee *Dynasphere Ranger—Dyna* for short!"

"A swell name!" Tom said, grinning.

After warm farewells, the boys prepared for take-off and soon the *Ranger* zoomed aloft with a steady blast of its repulsion beam.

The astronauts shot upward mile after mile. Soon the atmosphere outside their craft thinned away. The sunlit morning sky darkened into the blue-black void of space. Stars glittered at various distances.

When they reached an altitude of five hundred miles, Tom guided the craft deftly into orbit. Then he locked the controls and turned to Bud.

"Okay, fly-boy. Let's go satellite fishing."

"Great! I can't wait to see you cast this electrostatic net of yours!"

They climbed to the observation dome and Tom began setting a row of dials on the dynasphere's control console. He explained to Bud that he was feeding their orbital position and that of the satellite into a sighting computer. "That will automatically aim the electrostatic field."

As he clicked a switch and twirled several knobs, the huge crystal sphere on the *Dynasphere Ranger's* tail glowed with a bluish-red radiance.

"What a sight!" Bud gasped in awe. Then he chuckled. "Looks as if we've hitched our Flying Junkwagon to a star! . . . What now?"

"Watch it bring home the bacon—I hope."

Minutes went by while the boys waited tensely.

"Skipper, I'm still wondering why you let Rakshi get off the *Sky Queen*," Bud remarked some time later. "Something tells me you had a reason."

Tom nodded. "I was curious to see if he'd go for the Pigeon Special or the helicopter."

Before Tom could go on, Bud leaped to his feet and pointed excitedly to a glittering object in the distance. "Here she comes, pal!"

The boys grabbed binoculars. To Bud's amazement, instead of looking pleased at the success of his device, Tom was staring aghast at the fast-approaching satellite.

"Is anything wrong?" Bud asked.

"You bet! This isn't our satellite, Bud!"

"*What?* Are you sure?"

"Positive. The baby we're after looks like an ocean buoy, with four winglike solar panels. This job has an octagonal instrument package with two blades sticking straight out and a dish antenna projecting below." Tom groaned. "I think we've snared a Brungarian satellite!"

"Brungarian? Wow!" Bud knew that this foreign power was an old space rival of America and the Swifts. Its cosmonauts had tried to seize the phantom satellite and had raced Tom to the moon. "How did it happen, skipper?"

Tom was already checking. "Just plain bad luck. Its orbital path must have crossed our field and we pulled in the satellite."

By now, the object was near enough to be seen clearly with the naked eye. It was hurtling closer to the *Ranger* second by second. Tom switched off power. He slowed the object with the repelatron catchers and with magnetic grapples hugged it neatly into place in the curve of the fuselage. Its aluminum struts and gold panels reflected the sun's rays with dazzling brilliance.

Tom studied the satellite from the observation dome. "Brungarian, all right. Must be the orbiting space lab they launched recently. Our trackers found out it failed to achieve proper orbit."

"What a mess!" Bud muttered. "The Brungarians may even blame their own failure on us!"

Tom's brain was working fast. Unless he could figure a way out of their dilemma, an international incident was likely to result! He hurried below and radioed George Dilling.

"Get me the full orbital data on this Brungarian baby—fast," he ordered, "especially what its *intended* orbit was to be. They published all the information before they realized the shot was a flop."

Within minutes, Dillon had received it from Enterprises' Data Storage Center and transmitted it to the *Dyna Ranger*.

"Thanks, George," Tom responded. "One more thing—ship a three-D telejector over to Fearing pronto, and have the boys in our video-film lab tape a big three-dimensional sign for me—in Brungarian. Get a pencil and I'll dictate the wording in English."

Bud grinned as he listened.

After signing off, Tom gunned *Dyna* into action and sped upward toward the correct orbital path of the Brungarian satellite. Reaching the proper altitude, he released the magnetic grapples and maneuvered the satellite precisely into position, using the repelatron catchers.

"Nice shooting, skipper!" Bud said.

In a moment the *Dynasphere Ranger* was plunging back toward earth. As they landed on Fearing, a truck driven by Arv Hanson sped up, bringing the telejector equipment.

"The news is already out, skipper!" Arv reported breathlessly. "The Brungarians were tracking you *and* their satellite, and they figured out right off what happened. You should hear their propaganda broadcast about Tom Swift pirating their super-duper space lab!"

Tom grinned calmly. "In that case, we'd better not keep them waiting."

With the equipment aboard, *Dyna* took off

again. This time Tom headed for an orbital position directly over the capital city of Brungaria. From here, he switched on his telejector and trained its beam earthward.

In the Brungarian capital, traffic halted and crowds gathered, craning their necks at the sky. A huge sign in glowing red, white, and blue letters had appeared, visible for hundreds of miles:

TOM SWIFT APOLOGIZES FOR ACCIDEN-
TALLY CAPTURING YOUR SATELLITE. YOUR
GOVERNMENT HAS NOT YET INFORMED
YOU THAT THIS SATELLITE FAILED TO
ORBIT PROPERLY AND THEREFORE STRAYED
INTO OUR EXPERIMENTAL FORCE FIELD.
TO MAKE UP FOR THIS MISHAP, WE HAVE
MOVED THE SATELLITE INTO ITS CORRECT
AND HOPED-FOR ORBIT. WE ARE HAPPY TO
DO THIS FAVOR FOR OUR BRUNGARIAN
FRIENDS AND TO BRING YOU THE BEST
WISHES OF THE AMERICAN PEOPLE!

Bud was laughing uproariously. "That'll teach 'em!" he said.

Mr. Swift was on hand to greet the young astronauts when they landed back at Fearing. "Congratulations, son!" he told Tom. "You've turned a near disaster into a propaganda victory for the free world! I'm afraid there must be some pretty red faces in Brungaria tonight. The whole world is laughing over what happened."

"Are they going to protest to the UN, Dad?"

"Not a chance." The elder scientist chuckled. "Our State Department is sure they'll be only too happy to let the matter drop. The Brungarian dictators are afraid that any protest may bring more direct news flashes from America!"

Next morning Tom and Bud soared aloft for another try at retrieving the dead American satellite. This time the test went off perfectly. Tom grinned with satisfaction as he brought the glittering space object to a gentle halt and grappled it to the Flying Junkwagon.

"So far, so good," he said. "Now if we can just get this—"

"Tom! Look!" Bud broke in excitedly and pointed off to the left.

A needle-nosed yellow rocket ship was zooming toward them from nine o'clock!

"It looks like the mystery ship!" Bud yelled. "The same one that plowed into the space wheel!"

Tom stared in amazement at the strange craft. As he whipped a pair of electronic binoculars to his eyes for a better view, a thin stream of fire shot out from its bow.

The fiery streak billowed into a huge glowing mass and sped like a meteor toward the *Dynasphere Ranger!*

CHAPTER XV

ROCKET CHASE

"NOT another attack!" Bud gasped.

"Get below!" Tom shouted. The boys scrambled to the flight compartment. Tom seized the controls and sent the *Dyna Ranger* streaking upward.

But the fireball, too, veered from its course and kept on racing toward their craft!

"The thing's homing on us!" Bud gasped.

Tom began to zigzag, plunge, and climb. His efforts were useless. The weird object mimicked every move of the *Dyna Ranger* and continued to streak closer! By now, the whole compartment shone with the orange-red radiance of the huge fiery mass. The boys shielded their eyes.

"What can we do, skipper?" Bud asked in a strained voice.

"There's just one hope!" Tom gritted. He swung around in the pilot's seat toward the duplicate control board for the dynasphere. "I'll see what effect our electrostatic field has on it!" His fingers flew deftly over the panel, flicking knobs and switches.

Both boys sucked in their breath as the glowing mass suddenly disintegrated! The fireball seemed to explode before their eyes, spraying out a million sparks and fragments.

"You did it, Tom!" Bud exclaimed hoarsely.

The fiery shower lit up the sky for a moment, then died away as the particles burned out and faded in the blackness of space.

In the excitement there had been no time to watch the enemy rocket ship. But a moving blip on their radar screen showed it streaking away.

"I'm going after that baby!" Tom said grimly.

In a few moments the yellow raider could be made out far ahead. Tom switched on the dynasphere again and trained it on their foe.

At first there seemed to be no effect. Then the distance between the two ships began to close.

"You're slowing it down!" Bud cried.

The gap narrowed more and more as the electron-jet effect worked against the rocket ship's forward motion. It was almost as if the craft were bucking a powerful space wind. The *Dyna Ranger* began to overhaul its quarry!

Suddenly a fiery blast of exhaust spurted from the rocket ship as its pilot gunned his engines. The craft seemed to leap forward and break loose from the dynasphere's invisible field.

Bud fumed. "We almost had him!"

"We could nail him just the way we're going," Tom replied. "A few more spurts of acceleration like that would probably burn up all his fuel."

"Well, let's do it!"

Tom frowned thoughtfully as he hunched over the controls. "We might be courting trouble, Bud. We don't even know that ship's nationality. If we knock it out of action, the owner country could call our move an act of war."

"That sneak fired on us first," Bud growled.

"It would be our word against theirs."

"What about the time they slammed into the space wheel? We can certainly prove that!"

"They could say it was an accident—that the ship was out of control," Tom replied.

"Okay. What *do* we do?"

"Trail this guy," Tom decided. "At least we can find the location of his secret base."

The *Dyna Ranger* pursued the yellow rocket ship relentlessly. Twice more Tom used the dynasphere to slow it down, forcing the pilot to burn up precious reserves of rocket fuel.

By now, both rocket ships were arcing over the Pacific. The enemy ship was descending fast and both craft were glowing red from the heat of air friction. As the boys sighted the Asian mainland, the fugitive dived steeply.

"He's aiming for the Himalayas!" Bud exclaimed.

A fiery blast spurted from the rocket ship!

Tom hastily consulted a map of Asia, then watched as the yellow rocket ship arrowed downward. "The base must be just north of Vishnapur. That peak he's heading for is Chogyal."

Fearing a missile attack, Tom made no effort to swoop lower for a close-up view of the secret rocket stronghold. But he noted the latitude and longitude on the automatic navigator.

Both boys were thoughtful and said little as their globe-girdling westward flight continued. An hour or so later, while passing over Europe, Bud snapped his fingers. "Hey, I forgot all about the weather satellite! Hope we didn't lose it, chasing that fireball pitcher!"

Tom flicked a TV monitor. "It's okay. Those magnetic grapples don't let go easily."

When the *Dynasphere Ranger* finally landed on Fearing Island, crewmen and technicians swarmed to the launching area for a look at the salvaged satellite. Tom and Bud were cheered.

Mr. Swift shook hands with them warmly. "Well done, boys! Tom, I don't doubt your invention will do as well on retrieving the Mars rocket."

"Let's hope so, Dad. But there'll be fifty million miles difference in the range."

Tom waited for the debriefing session that followed in his father's island laboratory, and then gave a full report of their encounter with the enemy rocket ship.

"I'd say you handled the situation just right, son. A wrong move could have triggered serious international trouble. We'd better inform the Central Intelligence Agency immediately."

Tom telephoned the news to Washington. Then, after hanging up, he turned back to his father.

"How soon do we tackle the Mars rocket, Dad?"

"That's up to the government space agency," Mr. Swift replied. "They'll want to evaluate this test and examine the satellite to check the field effects on its transponders and magnetic data tapes. Probably in a week."

Tom bounced up excitedly from his chair. "With luck, that'll leave time enough for me to drain the Lake of Kali!"

The next day, back at Swift Enterprises, Bud found the young inventor hard at work in his laboratory. Tom was frowning over a bubbling mass of purple goo that was perking through an apparatus of chemical retorts and coils.

"The mad scientist himself," Bud remarked. "What sort of a witch's brew are you cooking up?"

"A valve to plug the lake inlet."

"A valve?" Bud echoed. "I don't see any hardware in that gunk."

"Not a metal valve. This is a colloidal solution of very fine particles that will set, or coagulate, into a gel."

The young scientist seemed so absorbed in his work that Bud gave up and walked out of the lab, looking puzzled. When he came back, late in the afternoon, Tom greeted him cheerfully.

This time, the setup on Tom's workbench consisted of a tall glass cylinder with a purple plug inside, about halfway down from the open top. Two insulated wires were connected to the plug through the glass wall of the cylinder.

"Let me guess," Bud said. "This is your valve and it's made out of that purple jelly."

Tom chuckled. "Right. But it's harder than jelly. I've named it 'electrogel.' "

"Okay. How does it work?"

Tom poured some water into the cylinder. It seeped quickly through the purple mass, which appeared to be porous. Tom opened a petcock at the bottom of the cylinder and drained off the water, then said, "Now watch what happens when I send a current through the plug."

He closed a switch and poured some more water into the cylinder. This time, the electrogel had become impervious to the water. Not a drop seeped through!

Bud watched in amazement. "Say, that's quite a trick! What's the secret?"

"The electricity polarizes the colloidal particles in a way that opposes any infiltration of water molecules."

Bud blinked and grinned. "Great! That tells

me nothing, but I'll take your word for it."

Tom explained that a huge quantity of the electrogel could be compressed into a small steel tank or cylinder for easy handling and then released underwater at the Lake of Kali inlet.

Preparations for the expedition were made by the weekend, and early Monday morning the two boys took off in the *Sky Queen* with Prince Jahan and the other student engineers. Due to time-zone difference, it was almost six o'clock in the evening when they swooped down over the Chullagar airfield in Vishnapur.

"Shri Swift," the tower operator radioed, "there is a man waiting to see you. Please come to the airfield office after you land."

The pilot and copilot exchanged puzzled glances. While Jahan and the others were disembarking with their luggage, Tom and Bud hurried to the office. The airfield manager, who had served in the Indian Air Force, met them at the doorway. "Your caller is inside, sir."

Entering the office, the boys saw a burly, fur-hatted Tibetan seated on the floor in a corner, sound asleep. The manager prodded him awake and explained, "He is a yak driver and came to Chullagar this morning with a caravan. Said he had an important message for Tom Swift—that he would give it to no one else."

The yak driver stood up, yawned, grinned, and pulled a folded piece of paper from his quilted

jacket. Tom read the message, then showed it to
Bud. The note was from Hugh Mortlake and
read:

> *I have information about the poison lake*
> *that may interest you. Chullagar radio says*
> *you are due back on Monday. Please call me.*

Tom paid the driver a handsome tip and hurried back to the *Sky Queen* with Bud. The boys
tried repeatedly to contact Mortlake over the
plane's radio but could get no response.

Tom frowned worriedly. "I hope nothing has
happened to him, Bud!"

When Tom explained the situation to Jahan,
the prince offered to fly with him at once to
Shankaru and investigate. With Bud they took off
in the *Queen*. When they reached the lonely site,
Tom hovered low over the ancient ruins but could
make out no sign of life below.

Alarmed, the three youths landed and began
searching among the crumbled fragments of the
long-dead civilization. They found the spot where
the archaeologist had camped, but his tent and
supplies were gone.

Suddenly Bud's face went pale. He pointed to a
heap of stones. "Something awful must have happened to Mortlake, Tom! Look over there!"

THE LAKE MONSTER

AMONG the stones lay Mortlake's radio, smashed beyond repair!

Tom, Bud, and Prince Jahan rushed over to examine it. The small portable transceiver had been pounded into a tangle of plastic, metal, and electronic parts.

"This is terrible!" Jahan said in a shocked voice. "He must have been attacked by bandits!"

"Why would bandits smash a valuable radio?" Bud objected. "They seem to have taken everything else—including Mortlake himself."

"Perhaps the men were superstitious and became frightened at the noise from the speaker," Jahan suggested, "so they broke it."

Tom looked grim. "You may be right." But he was not convinced that Jahan's theory was correct. "We might have a clue to the mystery if we knew what Mortlake wanted to tell me."

The young inventor recalled Rakshi's angry outburst when he had learned that the archaeologist was coming to Shankaru. Did the crumbled ruins hold some secret connected with the spy plot? Perhaps Mortlake had stumbled on the secret and paid with his life!

On the other hand, the information mentioned in Mortlake's letter referred to the Lake of Kali. Was it just a coincidence that he should disappear before he could tell Tom what he had learned?

"We must inform my uncle of this at once," Jahan said.

By now, dusk was beginning to close in over the eerie spot. Shivering, the three youths climbed aboard the Flying Lab and flew back to Chullagar. The other trainees had already gone to the palace.

At dinner Gopal assured Tom he would investigate fully the fate of the missing American. "I fear this is another sign of the dangerous unrest in Vishnapur," the dewan added.

"By the way," Tom said, "I understand that Rakshi was deported back to this country."

"Yes," Prince Gopal said. "So far he is being stubborn—but we have methods to insure that he will talk sooner or later."

Next morning a radio message picked up by the *Sky Queen* informed Tom that his diving seacopter, the *Sea Hound,* was on its way and would proceed straight to the Lake of Kali. This sleek jet craft could operate in the air and under the sea. A reversible rotor, enclosed amidships and spun by atomic turbine, enabled it to hover like a helicopter or plunge to the deepest ocean trenches. Tom had purposely not flown it to Vishnapur so the trainees would not see the top-secret underwater gear which the seacopter carried aboard.

Tom and Bud took off with Jahan's group in the *Queen*. As they swooped low over the lake valley, Bud exclaimed, "There's the good old *Sea Hound!* That hot rock, Arv, beat us."

Soon the two boys were shaking hands with the hulking, genial craftsman from Enterprises.

"Don't know if you've met Arv Hanson yet," Tom said, introducing him to the trainees. "He's our machine-shop maestro in charge of turning blueprints into pilot models. Arv, did you bring those electrogel tanks?"

"Sure thing, skipper. And the spectromarine selector, too. They're all in the seacopter."

"Doc" Simpson, Enterprises' young medic, greeted the boys. Then Chow's roly-poly figure elbowed forward with a grin. "An' I'm right here to dish up some poison lake fish, boss!"

Tom chuckled. "I'll bet you could do it too!"

The young inventor decided to let Prince Jahan make the dive with him and Bud on the *Sea Hound* while the other students observed from shore. He ordered a sonarphone with a loudspeaker to be set up on the beach so the onlookers could listen to a running account of what was happening below and also ask questions.

As the gear was being rigged, Tom outlined his plan of action to the students. He explained how he and Bud would leave the seacopter, wearing electronic hydrolung suits, and plant the cylinders of electrogel.

"But, Swift Sahib, are you not afraid of the poisonous water?" Tundup asked anxiously.

"Our suits should protect us," Tom replied. "The hydrolung gear will manufacture our oxygen supply, and we'll be encased in plastic."

Presently the *Sea Hound* took off and hovered out over the deadly lake. Arv brought the ship down gently. Then he eased the control wheel forward and the seacopter began her plunge as everyone stared through the big quartz pane.

"Boy, this water's really murky," Arv muttered. "I'd better turn on our beam."

Waving fronds and tendrils of the plants which had poisoned the lake could be seen all around. Fifty feet down, the growth was so thick Tom became alarmed.

"Better not go any deeper, Arv, or we may foul our rotors. Hover here, while Bud and I go down the rest of the way in our suits."

They donned their hydrolung gear of black plastic with torpedo-shaped drive jets in back and antennaed hoods. Each boy took a tank of electrogel under one arm and started out through the ship's air lock.

"All set, chum?" Tom asked by sonarphone.

"Right with you, fish-boy!" Bud chuckled. "This'll be like diving into a sea of spinach!"

Pressing their density controls, they started downward, groping their way among the weeds. Their suit lights shed yellow cones of radiance through the gloomy water.

"We're in a regular jungle down here," Tom reported to the students on shore. "No signs of fish or any other underwater life, except the plant growth. The lake inlet should be directly below us."

Moments later he went on, "Yes, I think I can see it now—a good-sized opening. Looks like a vertical channel about ten feet in diameter, straight down through bedrock."

Bud's voice cut in sharply over the sonarphone. "Tom! Over there—look!"

Tom turned his head. Through the murky waters he could make out a weird form. "Good night! It's the lake monster!"

A babble of excited queries came over the sonarphone, both from the *Sea Hound* and the students on shore.

"Can't see it too well," Tom reported slowly. "Four limbs, I think. . . . Yes. . . . Seems to be scaly. . . . Two large round eyes. . . . Doesn't seem aggressive—just watching so far. . . . Luckily there's a fair amount of jungle growth between us if—if—"

Tom's voice trailed off. His head was spinning. A wave of nausea swept over him.

"Skipper! Are you all right?" Arv called.

"Yes . . . I'm okay," Tom replied. "Feeling a bit sick, though. The poison in the water must be getting through into our oxygen systems!" Suddenly he jerked around. "Bud!"

As he spoke, Tom began stroking his way, one-handed, toward his partner.

"D-don't worry. . . . I'm all right," Bud responded. "But whew! I sure feel w-woozy!"

"I'm coming down after you!" Arv phoned.

"No need. . . . We can make it, I th-think."

Flicking their density controls, the boys bobbed upward—clawing aside the weeds. In a few moments they sighted the seacopter. The air-lock hatch opened to admit them, and soon eager hands were helping the boys into the cabin.

"Thank goodness!" Bud murmured, and Tom said, "Thanks."

Doc Simpson took charge immediately. After examining and treating Tom and Bud, he ordered both to rest.

Luckily only minute traces of the poison had filtered into their hydrolungs, and neither Tom nor Bud suffered more than passing effects. In an hour they were eager for a second try at plugging the lake inlet.

"This time we'll use Fat Man suits," Tom said.

This type of diving gear consisted of a huge steel egg, gyrostabilized, with a quartz glass window and mechanical arms and legs. The operator sat inside and worked the Fat Man's limbs through an electronic control board. Tom had invented the ingenious deep-sea escape gear while building his jetmarine.

The Fat Men had elaborate oxygen supply and purifying systems. The thick steel shells would protect them in case of attack by the lake monster. As an extra safeguard against the poison, Tom added special filters.

This time the two young divers started out from shore. The Vishnapurian students grinned and applauded as the steel-egg Humpty-Dumpties waddled out into the water. Each carried an electrogel tank in one mechanical arm and powerful cutters in the other in case of entanglement by the jungly underwater growth. Tom's Fat Man also carried two insulated cables which unreeled from a drum on the beach.

Tom kept up a running account over the sonarphone speaker. Twenty minutes later he reported, "We're at the lake inlet again. . . . Bud, plant your tank on that ledge below the opening. Mine can go in this niche. . . . Okay, open the tank valve. . . . The stuff's foaming out now, filling the inlet channel with purple gel. It'll set and be stiff in a few minutes. Meantime, I'll insert these cables. When they are connected to a D.C. source and the power is turned on, the plug should be watertight."

Finished, the boys rose. Jahan asked if they had glimpsed the monster again.

"Not a sign of him," Tom replied.

Back on land once more, Tom and Bud squirmed out of their suits and Tom connected the cables to one of his solar-charged batteries.

"Try calling the *Dyna Ranger* on radio," he told Arv Hanson. Arv did so from aboard the *Sea Hound* and presently reported that the salvage craft would arrive in an hour or so.

Tom and Bud ate a quick lunch and waited restlessly. At last the spacecraft was sighted, zooming down toward the lake. It landed and Hank Sterling climbed out.

"How're we doing, skipper?" he asked.

"So far, so good, Hank. We're all set to boil the lake dry!"

CHAPTER XVII

KALI'S SECRET

THE *Dyna Ranger* climbed steeply as Tom, at the controls, poured power to the repelatrons. The figures below became specks and the Lake of Kali shrank to a dark-greenish pool. Chogyal, with its icy ranges, stretched to the north.

"How high are we going, skipper?" Bud asked.

"Just high enough for a good angle with the sun," Tom replied. "This should do it," he added a few moments later.

Setting the controls, Tom started up to the observation dome. Bud followed. Topside, Tom sighted the sun's altitude, took bearings on the lake, then fed the information into the dyna-sphere's aiming computer.

Tom's fingers moved back and forth over the electronic console, flicking switches and twirling voltage controls as he conned the dials.

Presently the ship's great crystal sphere glowed

bluish red. Tom tuned it to infrared frequency. A vast, curving electrical field began to deflect solar heat rays onto the lake.

"Okay," Tom murmured tensely. "Now break out the electronic binoculars."

Within minutes, wisps of vapor could be seen rising from the lake's surface. The boys gazed down in fascination. The wisps became spouting columns of steam, roiling the lake into a seething caldron. In an hour the valley was almost hidden under the billowing vapor clouds.

"The level's down at least ten feet," Arv radioed. "Boy, what a fantastic spectacle!"

Hour after hour the lake continued to boil under the intense radiation. Tom shifted the ship's position several times as the sun sank lower. Late in the afternoon Arv reported that two-thirds of the water had boiled away.

As Tom gunned the repelatrons for more altitude, Bud asked, "Think we'll finish by sundown?"

"Sure. We'll go as far up as necessary to keep the sun's rays in focus."

Gradually the steam clouds began to thin out, and at last Arv radioed that the lake was dry. Jubilantly the two boys zoomed down and landed near the shore. The student engineers cheered.

"Magnificent!" Jahan told Tom. "The greatest scientific feat ever seen in Asia!"

"Thanks, but the job's not finished yet." Tom

grinned modestly and strode to the beach with
Bud to view the results of their work.

Daylight was fading, but the boys could see well
enough to be breathless at their accomplishment.
The entire lake bottom lay exposed. The weedy,
poisonous plant growth had sunk downward as the
water evaporated. Tangled, matted layers of the
stuff now covered the immense basin, which
sloped down sharply from the rocky shores to the
plugged inlet.

"Wow! That's a lot of gunk!" Bud muttered.
"Can you clean it out?"

"May take a while, but I don't see why not."

"What'll you use?"

"The thing Chow named the organ."

The de-organic-izer, dubbed "organ" for short,
was Tom's spectromarine selector. The young
inventor had built this machine to strip away the
barnacles and slime from the undersea city of gold,
which he had discovered while cruising near the
Atlantic Ridge.

"There's something interesting up near the
north end of the lake," Hank Sterling said. "Looks
like an underwater formation."

Tom looked where Hank was pointing. A curious cluster of high, bumpy protuberances thrust
upward from the bottom of the northern slope.
But plant growth covered them too thickly to
make out what lay beneath.

Tom gazed at the odd sight intently. "Let me

use your binoculars, Arv," he said, a note of suppressed excitement in his voice.

As Tom took the glasses and studied the formations, a strange thrill shot through him.

"What's under there?" Bud asked, puzzled, using binoculars himself. "The monster's lair?"

"I have an even wilder hunch, Bud!" Tom exclaimed. "Is the organ set up yet, Arv?"

"Sure, it's all assembled. But you're not going to tackle the job now, are you? It'll be dark in another fifteen minutes."

"We can work under floodlights."

"Now listen, boss, I got the vittles almost ready," Chow broke in.

Tom grinned and patted the cook's shoulder. "Okay, old-timer, lay it out while we're rigging the lights and we'll pitch right in."

Tom's eagerness spread to the others, and everyone assisted in setting up a row of powerful floodlights along the lake shore directly opposite the mysterious formations. A hasty meal followed aboard the *Sky Queen*.

Chow fumed. "Brand my biscuits, it's a waste o' time cookin' good grub if you're goin' to gulp it down like a pack o' coyotes!"

The boys grinned and hurried outside. They climbed aboard the spectromarine selector, with its operators' platform mounted on tractor treads. In front was the control pedestal with a cannon-like tube projecting forward. A vacuum hose was suspended from an overhead boom. Through the hose the gases from the cracking process were drawn aft into tanks.

Tom threw the engine into gear and the selector rumbled along the shore toward the spot where the lights had been set up. A white brilliance shone out across the lake bed.

Doc Simpson made his way through the group of students and technicians who had gathered to watch. "Here! Strap on these oxygen masks," he told the boys. "The air out there among all that poisonous gunk may not be too breathable."

Tom and Bud donned the oxygen gear and started out over the lake bed. The heavy tractor ground its way downward over the thick, slimy carpet of plant growth. Tom steered within the beams of light until they reached the nearest formation, and then maneuvered the machine into working position on the slope.

"Man! Whatever's under these weeds is huge!" Bud remarked, pulling aside his mask to speak. "The tops of these formations must reach up to within twenty feet of the surface."

Tom switched on power, aiming the unit at one towering mass. A hum came from the machine as the matted growth began to disappear as if by magic. Suddenly Bud clawed off his mask.

"Jumpin' jets! It's a building!"

Tom nodded, his own eyes blazing with excitement. His hunch, prompted by memories of the city of gold, had turned out to be correct!

As more and more of the wall surface came into view, the boys were astounded by its richness. It was made of gleaming white alabaster, inlaid with blue lapis lazuli and carnelian, and carved with fantastic figures of gods and demons. Tom switched off the de-organic-izer.

"There must be a whole group of palaces and temples under here!" Bud exclaimed.

"Right," Tom agreed. "This spot must have been engulfed by a flood centuries ago when the underground river bored that channel up into the valley. Bud, unless I miss my guess, this is the lost civilization of Vishnapur!"

"But I thought Shankaru was the site of—" Bud paused. "Say! Do you mean this place and Shankaru were part of the same civilization?"

"The wall carvings look similar, although what's left at Shankaru didn't seem as rich as all this," Tom said. "Shankaru may have been built later—and there may be inscriptions in the ruins telling about this place. If Mortlake deciphered them, that could have been what he wanted to tell me."

"Wow! I'll bet you're right!" Bud burst out. "And maybe someone wanted to stop him from—"

"Hold it!" Tom cocked his head. "Do you hear that noise?"

Bud listened for a moment. "I sure do."

*The machine rumbled downward over
the slimy lake bed*

The faint rumbling sound grew louder.

"Good night!" Tom muttered. "I wonder if anything's happened to the inlet plug." He turned to the watchers on shore and shouted, "Move the lights to bear on the center of the lake!"

The men leaped into action. Without waiting, Tom revved the tractor engine and began steering the spectromarine selector down the slope toward the center of the lake bed. The machine's own worklight beam stabbed the darkness ahead.

"What're you going to do, skipper?" Bud asked.

"This mass of weeds may have dragged the wires loose from the electrogel," Tom replied. "If we don't reconnect them in a hurry, the whole lake basin could flood again!"

Both boys were tense as the tractor rumbled forward. "Wish we could see a little farther," Bud said. "Doesn't look as if much water has seeped in yet, but—"

He broke off with a cry as the platform suddenly tilted forward. A second later the whole machine toppled down into the weeds. The boys could feel it sinking under their feet!

"We've hit a drop-off!" Tom shouted. "These plants must be afloat in water already!"

His last words were choked off by the rising flood. The boys struggled wildly, far from shore, in the tangled poisonous plant growth!

CHAPTER XVIII

HIDDEN LAIR

"PUT on your oxygen mask, Bud!" Tom yelled. He hastily adjusted his own before any of the deadly water could enter his mouth or nostrils.

In a moment the glare of the floodlights swept the center of the lake. Tom could see Bud floundering desperately in the morass.

Though both boys could swim like seals in open water, this ability would help them little until the lake level rose. For the time being they must fight to stay afloat in a seething stew of vegetation that was more like quicksand.

The matted weeds entangled their limbs like a net. Tom clawed out right and left and kicked his legs to keep from sinking, but every stroke increased his feeling of helplessness. Twice he saw Bud's head go under; then reappear moments later, with a look of sheer panic distorting Bud's face.

Suddenly Tom heard the whir of the *Sea*

Hound's rotor. A cone of light from the sky was moving out over the lake, with twin red and green running lights above. Then the craft's outline could be seen through the darkness.

"Thank goodness!" Tom muttered.

With rescue near, the boys struggled with new vigor to stay afloat. Soon a ladder was dropped from the *Sea Hound*. Tom motioned Bud to go first, then followed him up the swaying rungs.

"Th-thanks, pals!" Bud's teeth were chattering as two pairs of hands pulled him aboard.

Tom came next. He saw Chow's and Prince Jahan's faces in a blur, as a wave of exhaustion almost overcame the young inventor.

"Brand my water wings, you two sure picked a miser'ble place to go swimmin'," Chow clucked.

Doc Simpson draped blankets around Tom and Bud, while Chow hurried off to make hot cocoa. Jahan hovered near as Doc checked the boys' conditions. Hank Sterling looked around anxiously from the controls. "Are they all right?"

"They seem okay, but a bit woozy," Doc said.

Tom remarked ruefully, "Guess I was crazy to drive the organ where I did, but I was hoping I could fix the plug before it was too late."

Inwardly Tom felt heartsick at the ruin of their work. The whole lake would have to be drained again, and salvaging the spectromarine selector might prove a grueling job in itself.

Bud tried to cheer him. "That lost civilization

we found makes up for a lot. I'll bet those buildings are full of treasures!"

Jahan and Doc grew round-eyed with excitement upon hearing of the fabulous discovery. Suddenly Hank cried, "Skipper! Look!"

Tom rushed to the pilot's window, followed by the others. Hank pointed down to the left. A glinting metallic figure could be made out just beyond the fringe of brilliance from the floodlights. It was scuttling up the weedy slopes of the lake bed toward the northwestern shore.

"I spotted it just as I was turning the ship around!" Hank said. He zoomed the craft downward, swiveling its search beam. The creature zigzagged frantically, but Hank pinned it squarely in the *Sea Hound*'s yellow glare.

"It's the monster!" Bud gasped.

The scaly thing glanced up for a moment, and the watchers in the seacopter caught the reflected glint of two round bright eyes. Then it darted forward, scrabbling on all fours.

Tom swung around toward the pudgy cook, who was just bringing mugs of hot cocoa. "Get me some dry dungarees, Chow—pronto!"

"Me, too!" Bud shouted.

The cook hurried off and came back in a few moments with clothes, sweat socks, and canvas deck shoes from a supply locker. The boys had already shucked their blankets and were stripping off their wet garments.

Meanwhile, Hank had swooped still lower. The fleeing creature was now scarcely a hundred yards from the *Sea Hound*. The ship's beam revealed a cavelike hole in the rock face bordering the shore. The monster scrambled toward it. Hank's cry drew Tom's attention just as the creature scuttled into the opening.

"Set her down right here on the shore!" Tom ordered. As Hank obeyed, he finished dressing and took a quick gulp of cocoa.

"What're you aimin' to do, boss?" Chow asked.

"Go after that so-called monster."

"Are you crazy?" Doc broke in, aghast. "That thing's big enough to kill a man!"

"I think it *is* a man," Tom retorted. As the others gasped in astonishment, he went on, "It sure *looked* human the way it moved—and that getup could be a fancy diving suit. I have a hunch that ghoul sabotaged the lake plug!"

"If you're right, skipper, the guy may be a maniac—a killer," Hank pointed out.

"Yes, and that's why I'm going in alone."

"Now hold on, boss!" Chow burst out. "Brand my stewpot, you ain't goin' nowhere without—"

"You heard me, Chow," Tom said firmly.

"I forbid you to go after that creature alone!" Jahan exclaimed. "As Crown Prince of—"

Tom held up one hand, "I'm the skipper of this outfit, so let's have no mutinies, please." He softened his words with a grin. "Your safety is the responsibility of Swift Enterprises."

"Come on. Let's get going," Bud said.

Tom gave him a comradely poke in the ribs. "Okay, fly-boy, you tag along. The rest of you stay here."

Hank knew better than to argue. He reached for a small portable repelatron. "At least take this, skipper. If monster-man gets rough, you can pin him with a repulsion beam."

"Good idea. I have a hunch that hole is a tunnel—maybe a long one. Give us an hour. If we're not back by then, you're in charge."

"Roger!"

After anxious handshakes all around, the two boys armed themselves with powerful flashlights and climbed out of the seacopter. They scrambled down the rocky shore and entered the hole.

"It's a tunnel, all right," Bud murmured, aiming his beam ahead. The dank, earth-walled passage sloped upward into pitch-darkness.

At first the boys were forced to proceed single file, but the tunnel gradually widened. Tom aimed his light at a trail of damp tracks. They were webbed and clawlike.

"Ever seen prints like those before?" he said.

Bud gave a low whistle. "I sure have! Those tracks in the snow that Gyong thought were an Abominable Snowman's."

After a while the tunnel broadened out abruptly into a large chamber. The boys halted, their pulses racing, every sense alert. They shone their beams about the cavern.

"Look!" Tom gasped suddenly. His light had come to rest on a scaly figure, lying motionless and spread-eagled on the floor.

"It's the monster!" Bud exclaimed. "What's happened to him?" Tom readied his repelatron and the boys rushed forward.

"Don't move!" a voice barked. Then a light flared behind them. As the boys froze, they heard a sudden hiss and saw a puff of smoke burst from the rock wall nearby. A hole had been drilled in the solid rock!

"You see what my ray device can do, so don't tempt me to fire it your way!" the voice went on. "Drop that repelatron, Swift!"

Tom obeyed, gritting his teeth with rage. He and Bud exchanged furious glances. Both had recognized the voice as Rakshi's! And both realized the "monster" had been used as a lure.

Now the grotesque form got up—standing on two legs. Its large, round eyes, the boys now saw, were glass lenses in a strange sort of diving helmet, through which two human eyes leered out at them. Its wearer pulled off his swim fins and then removed the helmet. This, like the diving suit, appeared to be of some lightweight but strongly reinforced plastic.

"Prince Gopal!" Bud exclaimed.

The dewan's mustached lips twisted into a mocking smile. "You weren't expecting a real monster, I trust. This diving gear was designed merely to frighten superstitious hillmen. Their fear rid me of snoopers—until Tom Swift came along with his stupid project."

"Which would have exposed those priceless ruins under the lake," Tom said coolly. "I imagine you've been looting the treasures they contain— without informing the Rajah."

"Yes, and having them sold outside Vishnapur at fabulous prices," Gopal admitted. "And you, my friend, are not going to spoil my game!"

Bud's eyes blazed. "So you're the one who had that Kali sign painted—to scare us off."

The dewan nodded. "And my agents stirred up that mob to alarm you still more."

"What happened on that tiger hunt was meant to do more than 'alarm' us," Tom gritted.

Prince Gopal chuckled. "Quite right. Rakshi loosened your howdah girth before you mounted, and later he fired those quills. Yet you persisted in your project. So I had to take other measures."

"Like sabotaging the lake plug tonight?"

"Yes. A clever move, was it not? It failed to destroy you, but it has wiped out your work and brought you into my trap." Gopal's eyes narrowed. "You weren't surprised to see me?"

"Not very—since Rakshi proved he can fly a

helicopter and you own the only one in Vishnapur."

Gopal scowled at his henchman. "You fool, Rakshi! No wonder you were caught."

"You hired me to steal the Swifts' scientific secrets," Rakshi whined. "How could I know those blueprints were part of a trap?"

Tom put in casually, "By the way, was that Kali pin connected with your spy setup?"

"It is the insignia of my agents. Luckily Rakshi acted fast in Bombay and hired men to steal back the pin given to your sister. But I still had to take steps to throw you off the scent."

"Including the fake arrest of your man at the Chullagar Trading Company?" Tom needled.

Gopal's face hardened. "You will soon learn more of our setup—if you live long enough!"

The dewan changed quickly into other clothes. Then Tom and Bud were marched out of the cavern and deeper into the tunnel as Rakshi kept them covered. The passage sloped upward and Tom guessed that it led into the mountains.

At last they emerged into a moonlit canyon where Gopal's helicopter lay waiting. The boys' wrists were tied, then the two were herded aboard. Gopal took off. He flew northward across the snowy crags and at last hovered down over a deep valley rimmed by high mountain peaks. Tom's eyes widened.

Below lay the enemy secret rocket base!

CHAPTER XIX

ROCKET ROOST

A glow of landing lights, switched on at the helicopter's approach, revealed the base's equipment. Tom could make out shadowy gantries, a bristling array of missiles, fuel tanks, blockhouses, and high-masted antennas.

Bud gasped as the helicopter descended. "There's the rocket ship we chased!"

The yellow craft lay poised on its pad, the needle nose pointing skyward.

"Who would suspect such a base high in the Himalayan snows—eh?" Gopal chuckled. "The only approach is by a pass from the north."

Armed guards met the party on the airfield and escorted them to a concrete building. Inside a small office a squat, burly man rose from his desk. He had flat Mongolian features and wore a drab tan uniform.

"Ah, Prince Gopal!" He glanced at Tom and

Bud. "You bring us two interesting visitors."

"The blond one, Colonel Chung, is Tom Swift."

Chung's slit eyes widened. "A prize, indeed! And a boon to our joint efforts!"

"We're American citizens and you have no right to hold us here!" Tom blazed at the officer. "What country do you represent?"

"That does not matter," Chung purred, "since you will not return to America, anyhow."

"Your base here is illegal," Tom persisted. "This is Vishnapurian territory."

"Correction, please. It is claimed by Vishnapur but belongs to our People's Republic."

"Your dictatorship, you mean!" Bud snorted.

The colonel smiled blandly. "In any case, the question will soon be disposed of when our ally, Prince Gopal, takes the throne of Vishnapur."

The boys were startled. Tom turned to Gopal. "So that's why you tried to frame Prince Jahan!"

"Had he been convicted there would be one less obstacle in my way," the dewan confessed. "I hope to take over peacefully. If not"—he gestured toward the base—"a missile attack can be launched against Vishnapur as a last resort."

His ruthless words sent a chill down the boys' spines. Seeing their faces, Chung grinned.

"Prince Gopal and my government have a most useful partnership. We sell his lake treasures via Hong Kong. In return, he was to supply us scientific data from Swift Enterprises—data to strengthen our missile power for war."

As Tom and Bud looked at each other in dismay, Gopal said, "And now, Colonel, Rakshi and I must return to Chullagar. I am sure you will treat your guests well."

"Were they searched for weapons?" Chung asked.

"The Swifts do not approve of carrying weapons, Colonel," Rakshi replied mockingly. "Our young genius was carrying a small repelatron, but I disarmed him of that."

"Excellent. Then the cords will be removed from your wrists presently," Chung told Tom.

Before leaving, Gopal conferred with the officer in whispers. Both chuckled. When the dewan and Rakshi had left, Colonel Chung took Tom and Bud for a tour of the missile base. He boasted that his technical experts had developed a powerful new rocket fuel based on the age-old Oriental knowledge of gunpowder.

"Unfortunately, though, much of our space technology is still in a rather crude stage," the colonel admitted. He pointed to the yellow rocket ship. "This craft has features unknown to Western spacemen. Yet its control and guidance gear needs much improvement."

"Is that why it crashed into our space station?" Tom asked dryly.

"Yes. Most regrettable. Both its steering equipment and its inexperienced crew were at fault." Chung smirked maliciously. "However, we plan to speed up our development by—shall we say?— *borrowing* equipment and technical secrets from other nations' satellites."

Tom gasped. "So you stole the American satellite that disappeared from orbit!"

"Quite right," Chung gloated.

He led the boys into a large wooden shed. In it stood the glittering *Ionos II,* partly disassembled. "It was plucked from the sky by our rocket ship— this time with no control failures."

The boys were furious. "How about that fireball attack on my new ship?" Tom asked.

"Your space retrieval device posed a threat to our plans," Chung explained, "especially since we wish to capture the Mars rocket. Now that we have you in person, you will be well rewarded if you lend your skill to our work."

"Not a chance!" Tom retorted.

Colonel Chung smiled coldly. "My government has most effective brainwashing techniques."

Turning to the guards who had trailed them, Chung hissed out orders. The guards saluted and prodded the boys with their rifles toward a small blockhouse. Here, Tom's and Bud's wrists were untied and they were shoved inside.

As the door slammed shut, the boys looked around the bare cell-like room, then started in surprise. A man sprang up from a cot.

"Mortlake!" Bud gasped.

The archaeologist was haggard and unshaven. After hearing the boys' story, he reported that he had been captured at Shankaru by Gopal and Rakshi and flown to the secret missile base.

"I came to Vishnapur," Mortlake explained, "because art objects from its ancient civilization had been turning up on the world markets. I hoped to trace their source. Then at Shankaru I deciphered an inscription telling about the city under the lake. That's the information I wanted to pass on to you, Tom."

"Which explains why Gopal had you kidnapped," the young inventor deduced. Suddenly Tom heard a buzz and pulled his pencil radio from the pocket of his dungarees.

"What a break!" Bud exclaimed. "You had that with you all the time."

Tom grinned. "Lucky I slipped this in my pocket when we changed clothes."

As he tuned up the volume, a voice came from the speaker: *"Henry calling Mr. Fixit!"*

"That's Hank's voice!" Bud said excitedly.

"Fixit to Hank. We read you," Tom responded.

"I'm in the *Dyna Ranger,* over the missile base," the engineer reported. "Are you down there?"

"We sure are. How did you ever find us?"

Hank said he had been greatly worried about

the boys, so he had waited only a short time before coming to check on them. He and Jahan had hurried through the tunnel and had heard the racket of the helicopter echoing through the passageway as it took off. Although they were mystified by the boys' abduction, Hank knew about Tom's discovery of the enemy missile base, and Jahan recalled how the *Sky Queen* had been fired upon during their survey flight. So the two had decided to do some scouting in the *Ranger*.

"I used the dynasphere's field to spot the base's radar search pulses and also to trap them so that they would get no reflection from us."

"Terrific, Hank!" Tom exclaimed.

"What do we do next, skipper?"

Tom's mind worked fast. "We're being held in a blockhouse," he replied. "I don't know yet how we can break out, but *if* we can, are you game to try picking us up?"

"Just say when and where!"

At that moment a key scraped in the door lock. A sudden look of inspiration flashed between Tom and Bud. The copilot darted behind the door a split second before it swung open.

In stepped a pug-faced sentry, cradling a tommy gun. As his jet-black eyes swept the room suspiciously, Bud moved like lightning. He kicked the door shut, grabbed the sentry around the neck, choking him. The man's eyes bulged.

Tom was on him in one leap, wresting the gun

from his grasp. Bud hurled the sentry to the floor, and in moments Tom and Mortlake were tying and gagging the captive with strips of bedding.

"Grab that flashlight from his belt, Bud!"

Bud did so. Then he eased the door open—first a crack, then wider—and peered out cautiously. "We're in luck!" the copilot reported. "No other guards in sight."

As Tom and Mortlake followed Bud outside, the base appeared dark and silent, except for lights in the Headquarters Building at the northern side. The trio darted off in the opposite direction. Tom noticed that the radar antennas were turning steadily, but there was no sign of sentries.

"They must figure no one can get in or out of this place except by air," Bud muttered.

Soon they were past the launch area and the last blockhouse. Tom strained his eyes toward the beetling cliffs ahead. The moon was clouded and he could see only dimly. Most of the cliff walls rose sheer from the valley, but one area seemed climbable and flattened to a brush-clad mesa two hundred feet above.

"Let's try to get up there!" Tom said.

The three fugitives began the steep climb. Panting, they finally reached the mesa. Tom radioed the *Dyna Ranger*, lurking high in the stratosphere. Tense moments passed as they waited for it to descend. At last Bud spotted the craft in the faint moonlight and flashed a signal.

The fireball burst like an exploding star!

Tom fidgeted anxiously. "Somehow this has all been too easy, Bud."

"How right you are, my dear Swift!" As the Americans whirled, Gopal's voice went on, *"Keep them covered with your ray device, Rakshi!"*

The trio stared in helpless fury as the dewan and his henchman stepped from the brush.

Gopal chuckled. "We thought you might be followed, and Rakshi suspected Swift would be carrying that pocket radio, so we tuned in. We waited here, in the most likely spot for an aerial pickup—and the guard was signaled to let himself be captured. Now your ship must surrender or you all will be killed."

Tom made a desperate decision. "Hank, clear out!" he shouted into the transmitter.

Gopal's face contorted with rage as the *Dyna Ranger* zoomed upward. But an instant later a streak of flame shot up from the base!

It shaped itself into a fireball and sped toward the escaping spacecraft!

Tom and Bud watched, breathless with suspense. A speck of light glowed in the sky.

"Hank has turned on the dynasphere!" Bud cried triumphantly.

The fireball seemed to burst like an exploding star. Flaming fragments rained down from the sky. Moments later, a blinding glare turned the darkness into daylight and a terrific blast shook the valley!

CHAPTER XX

PLANET PRIZE

ABOARD the *Dyna Ranger*, Hank and Prince Jahan were white-faced with dread.

"What happened?" Jahan gasped.

"The base's rocket fuel tanks exploded!" Hank replied. "They must have been ignited by the hot debris from the fireball!"

"But Tom and Bud and Mortlake—"

Hank shook his head fearfully. "I don't know." He spoke frantically into the microphone, *"Dyna Ranger* calling Tom! . . . Tom!"

There was no response. Grimly silent, Hank swooped down toward the gutted rocket base.

Five bodies lay tumbled about the mesa. All had been knocked flat by the concussion from the tremendous blast. A lean, blond figure in dungarees was the first to stir. He raised his head dazedly and stared at the valley below.

Fires were blazing out of control, lighting the ruins of the enemy base. The blockhouses were still intact, but gantries and missiles had been ripped into tangled wreckage. Every wooden building had been leveled by the blast and the rocket ship had been blown to bits. The frantic personnel could be seen running about wildly.

"Good night!" Tom sprang up and looked around. By now, the others were regaining consciousness. Tom snatched up Rakshi's ray weapon, then shook his two companions.

"Bud! . . . Mortlake! . . . Snap out of it!"

Some sixth sense made Tom whirl just as Rakshi was about to spring on him. "Oh, no, you don't!" A lightning kick sent the plotter flying over backward.

Tom leveled the ray device at both Rakshi and Gopal. "Get up—both of you!" As they obeyed, glaring with hatred, Tom went on, "Now turn around. Bud, tie them with those ropes they brought to use on us!"

"It'll be a pleasure."

Soon the *Dyna Ranger* landed on the mesa. Tom and his companions prodded their prisoners aboard and the spacecraft soared into the night sky.

"I'm sure glad those sneaking skyjackers will get nothing out of the *Ionos II*," Bud said, looking down at the devastated base. "It must've been shattered."

Tom agreed. "And my repelatron in the helicopter, too."

Prince Jahan was stunned and angered upon learning of the treachery of his uncle. "My father will deal with him and Rakshi very severely," he told Tom.

The *Dyna Ranger* returned to the Lake of Kali, now completely flooded. At daybreak the prisoners were flown to Chullagar. Rajah Krishna listened sternly to Tom's report, then sent Gopal and Rakshi to prison to await trial.

"We shall protest to the United Nations at once about this perfidious attempt to cow Vishnapur with a missile base on her own border," he told Tom, who was standing by with Prince Jahan, Bud, and the other Americans. The bearded ruler went on grimly, "The world's atomic powers will make very sure, I think, that our neighbor has no second chance to plunge Asia into war."

After a late breakfast at the palace, Tom's group flew back to the Lake of Kali. Tom and Bud donned Fat Man suits and soon rewired the electrogel plug.

Then the boys took off in the *Dyna Ranger* to beam down infrared radiation. By sunset, the lake was once more boiled dry. Next morning the spectromarine selector was salvaged and restored to working order, and the job of removing the poisonous plant growth was begun.

During the afternoon, Arv Hanson brought

Tom a radio message received from Chullagar. It said that Rakshi had talked freely in hopes of lightening his punishment. He had confessed to recruiting Susak for the spy setup in New York and to planting the bug in Tom's lab. But apparently he had gleaned little information of value at Swift Enterprises. The clerk Chandra at Mukerji and Sons had been arrested by the Indian police, and a roundup of Gopal's agents in Vishnapur was now taking place.

Work at the lake proceeded rapidly with shifts manning the selector around the clock. By Saturday morning the ancient buildings had been thoroughly cleaned and the poisonous growth removed from a wide area of the lake bed.

Rajah Krishna arrived at noon with his Rani and members of the court. They lunched aboard the *Sky Queen* and viewed the results of Tom's work. The royal party stared wide-eyed at the alabaster temples and palaces gleaming in the bright Himalayan sunshine. Later, they toured the buildings and saw the decorations and treasures inside.

Finally Tom said, "My father has radioed that I'm needed back in America for the Mars rocket project. But a fresh crew of engineers is on their way here. While the lake bed is being cleaned, they'll lay pipes and dredge irrigation channels so the valley can be turned into farmland without submerging these buildings."

"Wonderful! Wonderful!" the Rajah said.

Before leaving, he rewarded Tom and Bud with priceless objects from the lost city. Tom received a jeweled dagger, and Bud the small statue of an archer carved from jade.

"Vishnapur owes you much, Shri Swift," the Rajah said. "These are only small tokens toward the full payment you have so richly earned."

By nightfall the boys were homeward bound in the *Sky Queen,* and on Monday morning scientists and officials from the government space agency conferred with Tom and his father on Fearing Island. Then Tom and Bud zoomed into space aboard the *Dyna Ranger.*

Ten thousand miles aloft, the boys went into orbit and climbed to the observation dome. Tom fed data to the aiming computer and began manipulating the switches and dials on the control console. The dynasphere shone with a bluish-red glow as it beamed its invisible field far out into interplanetary space.

"Nothing more we can do now. We'll just have to wait," Tom said. "The flight of the Mars rocket back to earth will take about forty days."

The two young astronauts returned to Fearing. During the anxious weeks that followed, Tom and Mr. Swift checked frequently on the rocket's progress over the megascope space prober. It appeared to be heading earthward on a true course. At last Tom and Bud soared aloft into space to intercept the Mars voyager. Like an arrow, the gleaming probe missile homed toward the dynasphere.

Bud watched breathlessly as Tom slowed their prize with the repelatron catchers and grappled it neatly to the *Dyna Ranger*. Then the copilot gave a wild whoop of triumph.

"You did it, pal! Nice going!"

Flushed with excitement, Tom hurried below to radio the good news to his father on Fearing Island. "Mission accomplished, Dad! We're on our way back to earth!"

"Well, what's your next big invention going to be?" Bud asked as his chum signed off.

Tom grinned. "I have several ideas cooking." He was already thinking of the priceless data to be gleaned from the rocket's instrument tapes and visualizing ways of using it to advance man's mastery of space. But the next invention from Tom's laboratory, his *Sonic Boom Trap,* would lead him into a totally different adventure, coping with a mystery of weird and dangerous sounds.

Bud chuckled. "I'm going to miss treasure hunting in space."

"Me too," Tom admitted. "Who knows— maybe someday the polar-ray dynasphere will bring in a new planet for us to explore!"